# September
# Song

Books by William Humphrey

WILLIAM
HUMPHREY

# September
# Song

Houghton Mifflin / Seymour Lawrence
*Boston · New York · London*

For information about permission to reproduce
selections from this book, write to
Permissions, Houghton Mifflin Company,
215 Park Avenue South, New York,
New York 10003.

*Library of Congress Cataloging-in-Publication Data*
Humphrey, William.
September song / William Humphrey.
p.    cm.
ISBN 0-395-58414-0
I. Title.
PS3558.U464S46    1992    92-896
813'.54 — dc20              CIP

Printed in the United States of America

HAD 10 9 8 7 6 5 4 3 2

*To my wife*

# CONTENTS

# A Portrait
# of the
# Artist as an
# Old Man

WAS IT JUST THAT, BEING YOUNG, new to her job, and an aspiring writer herself, she was in awe of an old one who had recently published, to some little long-overdue acclaim, his twelfth book? Was that what made her ill-at-ease? She had driven all the way up from the city to interview him, they had had drinks, lunch, and she had yet to ask him a question. It was as though he were interviewing her.

Not that there was much to tell about himself. Most of his 64 years had been spent at a desk, much of that time staring at a blank sheet of paper. How many writers' lives were colorful? Villon. Byron. Rimbaud. Poets. They left wide margins. The novelist, said Auden, must become the whole of boredom. Asked why he did not write an autobiography, Thomas Hardy replied that he was not much interested in himself. As for him, he had never bothered answering inquiries from *Who's Who*. List the titles of his books, and his tale was told.

But he was prepared now to help his reluctant young interviewer with the information that he was born in Sulphur Flats, Texas, in 1924. Had attended the local schools until his father's death in 1937 when his mother and he moved to Dallas. There he finished public school and then enrolled on a scholarship at Southern Methodist University. In 1945 he came to New York

where he met and married his wife. Published his first story in
1949, his first book in —

Then he knew what this reporter was here for and why she
was hesitant at her assignment. His twelve books had earned him
an obituary in her newspaper — on a back page, of course —
and his age made it urgent to get the facts on file. Here was
Death in the guise of a young woman.

The little black box with its tape cassette used by today's Recording Angel posed a challenge. His wife listened in blank-
faced amazement as he began the story of his life with:

"My mother having died in giving birth to me, her only child,
I was brought up by a black mammy. Do not picture a Dilsey
or an Aunt Jemima. Mammy was just fifteen years older than I.
My bereaved father had to have a wet-nurse for his motherless
child and Mammy's pappy, a Holy-Roller minister, had kicked
her out of the house when she showed signs of becoming a
single parent. I never knew Mammy's pappy but he had a de-
cisive influence on me. It is to her resentment of his treatment
of her that I owe my having been brought up in a godless
household, for which I have always thanked whatever powers
there be. As I required constant attention, she moved in with
us. Of course she went in and out the back door, and it goes
without saying that she 'mistered' my father, still, her living
in the house with a single man, and with her tarnished reputation, must have raised eyebrows in our little old southern town.
But whatever gossip it may have caused was not repeated to
my father's face because of his well-known prowess with a gun,
about which more later. It did mean that I grew up sheltered.
We never had company in the house. It was perhaps the beginning of my lifelong sense of alienation.

"At one flowing breast Mammy nursed me and at the other
her Josh. So, although he and I later went our separate ways,

we started life side by side. Until I was six years old and my education began, I thought Mammy was my mother. All reminders of my own had been removed from sight so as to prevent any questions and spare me the knowledge of my congenital parricide. I could see of course that there was a disparity in color between Josh and me but I thought he was Mammy's black boy and I her white one. Because he resembled her more than I did, I deferred to him and he took advantage of that to lord it over me.

"My first day of school was a turning point in my life. My being taken to one and Josh to another opened my eyes to the difference between us. My teachers were scandalized by my dialect and asked where I had learned to talk like that. If you think I've got an accent now you ought to have heard me recite my bedtime prayers, taught to me by Mammy not out of piety but out of superstition: 'Now Ah lays me down to sleep / Prays de Lawd mah soul to keep.' My teachers made me feel peculiar, which is to say inferior, and that made me question my upbringing. My life had not been so secluded that I had never seen white mothers but I had never seen them in such numbers as came to fetch their children when school let out that day — and waiting for me was Mammy. My white hand and her black one holding it as she led me home had never looked so mismatched.

"'Mammy,' said I in a flash of divination over my Graham crackers and milk, 'you're not my mother.'

"'Nevah said I wuz!' she rejoined indignantly.

"Wouldn't have you as a gift, was my reading of that.

"Remember the sad old song 'Sometimes I feel like a motherless child.' Well, just imagine what it's like to lose in one moment both of yours. It may have been then and there that my métier was decided for me. You've heard no doubt of that modern literary theme 'The Quest for the Father.' Mine was for the mother. 'The Anna Fisher Obsession' it's called. I couldn't look at a white woman of child-bearing age without wondering whether ... And wondering what I had done to make her disown me.

"Mammy knew the truth kept from me about my unfortunate origin, but she knew better than to tell white folks what they did not want to hear about themselves. Only one person could clue me in my search.

"So that I might look upon myself as an accident rather than as a born criminal worthy of hounding by the Furies, it was necessary that I be precociously initiated into the facts of life.

"'So you see, son,' said my father in concluding his anatomy lesson, 'it was not your fault.' But his look of profound pity for me was like the mark of Cain upon my brow.

"Top that up for you, Miss?

"Separate but equal, we called our segregated school system. Everybody now knows that was a sham. I learned it earlier than most. My teachers were old maids — forbidden by law to marry. This left them free to turn all their attentions upon their pupils. Their attentions, I say, not their affections. For the next seven years I was sent home each afternoon staggering under the load of my homework. One hundred complex compound sentences to diagram. One hundred problems of long division to solve. My studies stunted my growth. I blame many of my afflictions and my disappointments in life on my unathletic childhood. Meanwhile Josh was out on his skates or his scooter or my bicycle. If you think he spared me the contrast between his freedom and my bondage, then you don't know kids, black or white. Imagine if you can what it was like to be a little overworked, motherless, guilt-ridden boy trying to memorize the poem assigned to him to be recited at morning assembly while a handball was being bounced against the side of the wood frame house."

"I'm going to need another tape," said the reporter.

You're going to need more than one, young lady, he said to himself. For inspiration — or desperation — or were they one and the same? — was upon him. "Is it not the sound the great wings make as Death swoops past that moves the soul to art?" Who wrote that? He did. And he was young then. He poured himself another drink. The reporter covered her glass with her hand.

"To say that my killing my mother as my first act in life benefited me in any way may sound callous, but surely it spared me the pangs of the Oedipus complex, and in my case that was to be the one ray of light. 'Oedipus complex?' a friend of mine whose mother was unattractive once said to me. 'I just took a second look.' Well, I never got a first look. Not so much as a snapshot. I was not jealous of my father. On the contrary, once aware of my awful guilt I felt beholden to him for having deprived him of his young and fertile wife. He might tell me it was not my fault, but I blamed myself all the same. It was just like me to come into the world ass-first and right-side-up instead of head-first and upside-down like every normal person. And though the dear man never gave me any reason to feel that he resented me, I felt myself to be a constant reminder to him of his loss and loneliness. He was obliged to support and to cherish the very agent of his bereavement. I was his albatross. He never remarried, and I blamed myself for that too. I made him undesirable as a husband. I bore him no ill will. Before the bar of eternal justice I can truthfully swear that I did not intend to kill my father.

"Freshen that for you, young lady? Sure? Well, I'm not driving.

"Ad Tupperwine: that is a name that may not be familiar to you. No. *Sic transit gloria mundi.* Ad Tupperwine was to the semi-automatic .22 caliber rifle what Rubenstein was to the keyboard, Babe Ruth to the bat. The greatest trick-shot artist of them all. Though in fairness to myself I must say he never took the risks I took.

"No, Ad Tupperwine is not remembered as is Buffalo Bill or Annie Oakley, but he was of that ilk. He toured the country with his road show generating publicity and sales for one of the arms manufacturers. After his visit to some cowtown the hardware store sold out of guns and ammunition. It was his visit to Sulphur Flats that prompted my father to take to the road in emulation of Ad Tupperwine when his business failed.

"I was emancipated from school. Until then I had been like a chick trying to peck its way out of its shell. On our tour we never stayed in one spot long enough for the local authorities to seize me and send me back to my textbooks. I was saddened to say goodbye to Mammy but glad to see the last of Josh. While I was slaving away at compulsory education he was a junior high school dropout and his color freed him from the attentions of the truant officer. How he did swagger in his liberty and idleness! He had become a bully and, I regret to say, a bigot. Mind you, I blame his prejudice on environment, not heredity, for a more tolerant person than his mother could not be found. He and I were raised as equals. When she weaned me she shut off Josh's tap too. If in fact she showed any partiality it was toward me because, knowing I had no claim on her maternity, I never sassed her.

"At first I was only my father's assistant. Like the organ-grinder's monkey. I tossed the glass balls into the air, he burst them. I set up the plaques on which, in bulletholes, he drew the cartoon characters, the kitchen matches he lighted with a shot and the candles he snuffed shooting backwards over his shoulder using a mirror, the nails he drove all the way into the board.

I passed the hat after the show was over. Even as nothing more than his helper I was the starry-eyed envy of every boy in our audience.

"But, disappointed by the size of the crowds we drew and in our gate receipts, my father had an inspiration. I went into training.

"I thought I had worked hard in school. No little musical prodigy deprived of a normal childhood by practicing his instrument from dawn to dusk ever applied himself more diligently than I did to that .22 rifle. We were now a father-and-son act. A comparison with the Mozarts, *père et fils,* or with the elder Picasso's giving his son his paintbrushes would not be amiss.

"The times were bad and getting worse by the day. Those were the Depression years and our territory was the Dust Bowl. We played to thin crowds and they were composed of dirt farmers, small-town tradesmen. We couldn't charge admission because we performed in cow pastures. Sometimes when I passed the hat afterwards we took in barely enough to pay for our ammunition.

"Now there was never any doubt that I was the star attraction of our show. Not because I was a better shot than my father but because I was a prodigy. Although I was fourteen, owing to my stunted development I passed for eleven. I was the boy wonder of the trick-shot circuit. So in looking for a way to improve our attendance it was natural that my father think of featuring me more prominently. To train for this we wintered down on the Rio Grande where the climate permitted me to practice nonstop. For I had to become not just a better shot than I already was — I had to become a perfect shot, no allowance for a miss. You will understand why when I tell you in a minute how I was billed.

"By spring I must have fired a hundred thousand rounds. I

attribute my present hardness of hearing to all that persistent shooting. Sounded like an agitated woodpecker at work on my eardrums. We headed north. We went on as before drawing the bullethole pictures, striking matches, snuffing the candles, bursting the balls in the air, but the grand finale featured me as William Tell, Jr.

"Take it from one who knows, Miss, the biggest apple in the world looks mighty small when it's sitting on your father's head and you're drawing a bead on it from fifty feet away. Father had the utmost confidence in me and that bolstered my self-confidence, still —

"I can tell by your look of expectancy and dread that you have anticipated my dénouement. Yes, alas, we tempted fate once too often. It caught up with us on a hot day in a hayfield outside Wichita Falls. After the fatal shot I got to him just in time to hear my father say, 'Son, it was not your fault.'

"My career as a trick-shot artist in shambles and I a self-made orphan twice over, hounded by guilt and remorse I joined the ranks of the homeless and became a drifter, fleeing from my memories yet compelled to tell my story to any and all who would listen. My wanderings were as driven and as aimless as those of eyeless old Oedipus only unlike him I was unattended by two devoted daughters. I was a teenage outcast. The account of my attempts to start life anew — well, you've got a deadline to meet. Let two stand for the lot. I got to be a good enough pool shark to take in the small-town players, fill my pockets with cash, get cocky, challenge the hustlers, and lose. My hopes of becoming the next Benny Goodman and forming a jazz band were disappointed when, after six months' dedication to the instrument, I was forced to acknowledge that I was not progressing because for me one note was one beat and one beat one note.

"And so, having failed at everything else I had tried my hand at, I took up writing.

"If I thought I had worked hard in school and at trick-shooting — !"

"Do you think," asked his wife when the reporter had departed, "that young woman believed a word of that rigamarole?"

"I thought I made it quite convincing. I was breaking my heart."

"You've had a sad enough life. You've told me about your poverty-stricken childhood. You've described to me with tears in your eyes watching your poor father die from his injuries in that automobile accident. You've told me about how they put your mother on roller skates so she could fill the mail orders faster at the Sears, Roebuck warehouse in Dallas, struggling to support the two of you on eleven dollars a week's pay. What satisfaction do you get out of making up for yourself an even worse life than the one you've had?"

"Makes mine more tolerable. And as long as I can make up one I'm still here."

"But what are you going to say to people who know you when that yarn appears in print?"

"I won't be here." And he then explained to her what the reporter's assignment was. "In the trade they're called 'ghouls' or 'buzzards.' She was here to gather material for what they call an 'advance obituary.' Somebody's got to do it, but it is dirty work. What I didn't tell her was my last words."

"Oh, you've got them ready, have you?"

"Mmh."

"What are they?"

"They're the last words of a writer: 'In that case, I've got nothing more to say.'"

# The Farmer's Daughter

THERE WAS NOBODY TRAVELING on the road nor working in the fields alongside to see the man fall off the telephone pole, for the day was the Fourth of July and the farmfolks had all gone into town for the celebrations. He had been replacing broken insulators on which boys liked to practice their marksmanship. He had just loosened his safety belt to descend. He fell without a cry, for he was already unconscious, having worked on to finish this job without going down to retrieve his fallen hat, something anybody should have known better than to do in the blaze of a Texas midsummer day, and had had a sunstroke. When he hit the ground he seemed to explode, the powdery dust bursting about him in a puff. He fell on his right leg, which broke with a crunch like a soda cracker. The climbing spur on his twisted foot, ripping through his trousers, tore the calf of his other leg. His head struck the base of the pole hard enough to make the crossarm quiver.

In a last convulsive movement before falling the man had clutched the wire. It broke where he had spliced it, the loose ends snapping back toward the adjacent poles fifty yards away on both sides. The birds perched upon the wire bounced into the air on the wave of the shock, twittering at the disturbance. As the vibration ceased and the ends of the wire dangled motionless, they flew back and alighted again. The disconnected pole stood like a cross above the prostrate figure.

The young man lay face up in the glare of the sun, yet he did not sweat. On the contrary, the sweat bathing his face when he fell, that icy eruption which comes, in sunstroke, as all the lights and darks are reversed and the world becomes a photographic negative, just before the loss of consciousness, had quickly dried, and his face, streaked with dirt, was now unnaturally cool-looking. His leg skewed in an inconceivable direction. His palms, black with creosote from the pole, were turned upwards as though in supplication. His breathing was so shallow his chest barely rose.

It was after noon when the man fell. His lunch pail sat at the base of the pole. Beside it and his fallen hat lay the book, a thick volume entitled *Torts,* which he had read while eating. A few grasshoppers clicked in the air. A terrapin, having struggled across the road only to come up against the wheel of the telephone company truck, turned and dragged itself back again. The man's face drained a shade paler and his jaw sagged, causing his mouth to gape.

The shadow of the pole lengthened and slowly semicircled, a sundial needle, throughout the long afternoon. Occasionally the man's throat commenced to work, trying to swallow. His eyelids opened, fluttered, then swooned shut again. His chest expanded, he gasped, and from his depths came a thick-tongued groan, a sound palateless and glottal such as deaf-mutes make.

From time to time the two-way radio in the truck crackled to life and squawked, "Jeff Duncan. Come in. Where are you, Jeff Duncan?"

After nightfall the holiday fireworks in the town erupted. Several times the injured man regained consciousness, only to lose it again shortly, which was merciful. For, as he would later tell his rescuers, it seemed to him that the explosions and the bursts of light were inside his head.

Cliff and Beth Etheridge took a proprietary interest in the young man whom they had found so badly injured, whose life they may have saved, all the more so when they learned that he was alone in the world, orphaned in his infancy. Having lost her mother just three years earlier, Beth marveled at anyone's courage and resourcefulness in bringing himself up without one. No breast to nurse at, none to cry upon! Their day's work done, father and daughter drove every evening to the hospital, their patient's only visitors.

The broken leg — broken in three places — remained in splints and a cast; it would forevermore be shorter than its mate. But the bandages had been removed from his head, and his hair, shorn for surgery, was an inch long, his beard twice that length, when the doctor said, "He could go home now, if he had a home to go to. He can't look after himself, but he doesn't have to stay here. And his workman's compensation is soon coming to an end." Cliff Etheridge had no need to confer with his daughter. "He's got a home with us," said Cliff.

The discharged patient was taken by ambulance to the farm, there carried inside on a stretcher. The Etheridges led the way in the pickup, bringing with them a wheelchair and crutches lent by the hospital. A bouquet awaited their guest and the television set had been moved into his room. Such kindness — not just from strangers, for everybody was a stranger to Jeff Duncan — left him tongue-tied. He was like a stray cat, grateful but mistrustful on being taken in, housed and petted.

The door to his room was left open for Beth to hear his call. At first, still on painkillers, he slept much of the day. She went about her housework noiselessly, peeking in on her patient from time to time, never without a pang of pity, sometimes a tear, for his injuries and for his lifelong loneliness, and a feeling of gratitude for being able to nurse him. Her father's unhesitating hospitality, though it was just what was to be expected of him, also produced an occasional tear, as did his certainty that she would concur. Later, when her patient was more alert, she felt called upon to sit with him, though she worried over what she might say that would interest a person so serious-minded and so well educated. Daytime television did not.

She was his only company, for at this season her father was in the fields from dawn to dusk. She wanted her patient to feel at home, welcome, not beholden. She wanted to make up for all the neglect he had endured. She looked in on him every few minutes, for he was so undemanding she had to thrust her attentions upon him. She had all but to woo him. Having been made to sit up and beg for every scrap of kindness, he did not bite the hand that fed him, but neither did he lick it.

"You've been to college," she said admiringly.

"You have to in order to get into law school," he said.

"I've never known anybody who's been to college," she said.

"You have if you've ever gone to a doctor or a lawyer," he said.

"We had the doctors with my poor mother," she said sadly. "But — knock wood — we've never had to have a lawyer, thank goodness. Oh! I didn't mean that the way it sounded." And she blushed.

"I hope you never have need of one. But if you ever do, call on me. Just manage to keep out of trouble for another few years. Then I'll get you out of any scrape."

"I suppose you speak French," she said.

"I studied it in school," he said somewhat warily. "Why?"

"To me being able to speak another language is like being

given an extra life. I've heard it said that every educated person speaks French."

"I have never had much use for mine. But then, I never expected to." It was an admission that caused him some embarrassment.

"Oh," she said impatiently, "does everything have to be useful? Can't some things just be beautiful? I was planning to take it in my junior year but when Mom died I had to drop out of school to look after Dad. I wouldn't have had anybody to speak it with, but that, if you can believe it, was one of my reasons for wanting to know it. It would have been something all my own. I might have written my diary in it. I expect you think that's silly."

He looked at her so closely and for so long that she said, "What is the matter?"

"What you just said," he said. "You might have been speaking for me."

Studying French had been his one deviation from the straight and narrow path he plodded down — or rather up. He ought instead to have elected Spanish. He might in time have some Spanish-speaking clients. But he wanted to know a language unknown to anybody around him, to belong to a select, almost a secret society. Institutionalized all his life, he had never known privacy. His very name seemed something conferred upon him for the convenience of his keepers. "I suppose you think that's silly," he said.

She did not even bother to answer. They understood each other, the only ones who could. French was a folly they shared.

"Speak some to me," she said.

He hesitated for a moment, then he intoned:

"*Les sanglots longs*
*Des violons*

*De l'automne*
*Blessent mon coeur*
*D'une langueur*
*Monotone.*"

The singsong cadence, the rhymes, the pitch of it brought to her mind the melancholy call of the mourning dove.

When the recitation ended, the words — if words they were and not musical notes — lingered on in a withdrawing echo. Wrapped in revery, she could say nothing for a while. Then she said, "Beautiful. That is beautiful. To think there is a country where people sound like that! Tell me now, what does it mean?"

He translated.

Again she was silent for a while before saying, "How sad. How beautiful."

She had him recite it so many times over the next weeks that she learned it by heart.

He was impatient to get on with his studies. He had no time to lose. He would soon be going back to school. He could not just lie idle.

But, "I don't understand what I'm reading," he said.

She took the book from him and scanned a page.

"Who could?" she said.

Then she regretted her flippancy. His expression was one of despair.

"When I fell off that pole I fell a long way," he said. "I was reaching for the stars."

She was the first person to whom he had ever confided his aspirations, and he could do so now only because they had been dashed. He had kept them to himself for fear that in him they would be thought presumptuous, preposterous. He was ashamed of being an orphan and beholden to all the world. She was flattered to be singled out as his confidant.

As a boy he had delivered groceries after school and on Saturdays. He had mowed lawns in summer, raked leaves in the fall. He ran errands for shut-ins. All that he earned he saved. He had neither time nor money for amusements. He came to be well known and he made himself well liked. Dependent upon charity, he learned early in life the worth of a smile. "That young fellow will go far," he overheard said of him.

He had a long way to go to reach the goal he had set for himself. But he believed then that nothing could stop him.

She listened to the story of his poor and joyless life, his lack of affection, of any true childhood, of a home, even a room of his own, and though she was years younger than he it appealed to her motherly feelings. She could see before her the earnest, unsmiling boy dressed in ill-fitting castoff orphanage clothes.

By dint of hard work he stood near the head of his class, and when he graduated this earned him a scholarship to college. He supported himself by working nights as a janitor, during the summer vacation as a telephone linesman. He had fixed his sights on a distant target, and he never lifted his eyes from it. Law school, the bar exam, legal practice, then . . .

He blushed for his immodesty. "Would you believe, I had dreams of someday being governor."

"You will! You will!" she said fervently.

"I will never climb another telephone pole. I can't work as a janitor anymore."

"You'll get a desk job."

"Not if my brain has been damaged, I won't."

He told of that last moment of consciousness before his fall when light was dark and dark was light, and it seemed to him that his world, once so sharp and clear, was that way now. He had lost his bearings.

"The head will clear up," said the doctor. He warned of atrophy of the muscles of the legs through disuse. As instructed, Beth suspended bags of sugar from her patient's ankles and he lifted and lowered them. He clenched his teeth in pain and the sweat stood out on his brow. He shook his head in discouragement.

"Five minutes more," she said. "You can do it."

When the time for it came she trained him to walk again without crutches. She exercised him like a drill sergeant making a raw recruit shape up.

"Come to me. Come to me," she coaxed, backing away and beckoning as he advanced.

Each step toward her was a step away from her. She likened herself to a bird teaching its young to fly, knowing all the while that it would fly the nest first thing.

Probably he was as near to loving her as anybody in his loveless life. That he was fond of her she could see. That he was not shy of showing it made plain how far it was from being anything more. They were friends, and there was no greater bar to love than friendship.

Yet she wondered whether his feeling for her ran deeper than he would allow himself to declare or even acknowledge. Obliged to work his way through school and attend classes part-time, he had years yet to go. Then he could not expect to attract clients at once. Perhaps he was shy of asking her to wait for him, thinking that it would be unfair to her, that some good man might propose to her and, bound by her promise, she lose out on him.

Their time together was drawing to a close. Soon would sound *les sanglots longs des violons de l'automne*. Harvest time had come.

She was busy in the kitchen putting up the garden produce. He was helping. While she sterilized jars and skinned tomatoes he sat at the table snapping beans. What neither was doing demanded concentration but they worked in silence. The snapping of each bean sounded like somebody cracking his knuckles.

Several times he rested from his labors and she observed him gazing out the window. He seemed to be rehearsing a speech and refining it.

"What did you say?" she asked.

He shook his head. "Nothing," he said, and went back to snapping beans.

But something, she felt, was simmering in him like the pot on the range. Again the snapping stopped and he cleared his throat.

"Yes?" she said eagerly.

He said, "I've been trying to find words —"

"Yes? Yes?"

"— to thank you for all you've done for me. You and your father."

"You don't need to," she said, and turned away to hide her tears of disappointment.

When the cast was removed he said, "Struck off my ball and chain."

She wondered where a person might get splints and a cast for a broken heart.

He would be going back to the rooming house which had been his home during the school session for years. He was already late for classes. He must make applications for a new job. His being crippled would only strengthen his resolve. He was sure to succeed. She would follow his rise from afar.

In preparation for his departure he sat in the yard wrapped in a bedsheet while she clipped off his beard. Unlike Delilah, she was not unmanning her Samson, she was grooming him to take on the Philistines. Clean-shaven, he was a different person, a stranger to her, and belonged to the outer world.

On the way to the depot the three sat on the single seat of the pickup, she in the middle pressed against him. Though ordinarily her father liked to let her drive them, a little mark of his confidence in her, today he drove. She sensed that he knew she did not trust herself to do it, that she had her thoughts to think. Looking straight ahead, they rode in silence while the seams in the pavement ticked as regular as a clock.

Up to the time the train pulled into the station she kept hoping without hope that he would ask her to wait for him. She would have had to nod her answer.

He shook hands for the last time with her father and gave her a peck on the cheek. He cleared his throat, and for an instant she thought he was going to say the word. He said goodbye.

Ahead of the train a wind blew down the tracks, sweeping before it an early-fallen leaf. She recited to herself:

"*Et je m'en vais*
*Au vent mauvais*
*Qui m'emporte*
*Deça, delà*
*Pareil à la*
*Feuille morte.*"

Like an executioner's order to fire, the conductor's cry rang out, " 'Board!"

She watched him limp across the tracks. She longed to call, "Come back! Come to me!" Before mounting the steps he turned and waved goodbye.

No sound was so sad and lonesome as the whistle of a departing train to one left behind.

# A Labor
of Love

THEIR MOTHER HAD HAD A CRAVING for sour pickles all the while she was carrying Berenice: that was how Henry Howard accounted for his sister's disposition.

It was not for sweets, that was for sure, his wife Susan, avoiding contractions for the sake of emphasis, agreed. And I do not believe Wendell's mother ever ate anything at all while she was carrying him: that was her explanation for their brother-in-law's disposition, or lack of any.

"Cut that man with a blade and I vow he wouldn't bleed. If anything flowed at all it would look like skim milk," she declared. "That woman has drained him dry of what little sap he ever had in him." Among Susan's many names for her sister-in-law one was the Praying Mantis.

"Wendell has never done anything but take up space," said Henry.

"He only knows two words," said Susan, and she quoted them, mimicking to perfection Wendell's mousy manner: "'Yes, Berenice.' When what she needed all along was somebody to whale the stuffing out of her."

Berenice now wrote that Wendell was at death's door.

"As somebody said of Calvin Coolidge," said Susan, "how can they tell?"

"She'll have nowhere to go," said Henry.

"Nowhere to go? She's got three grown children. Though how she managed it I don't know, except like the Virgin Mary."

"They wouldn't keep her in their doghouse."

"So now at your age you're going to build her a home."

"I'll get Junior to help me."

"When? After he has already put in a day's work at the mill? On his Sundays off? A lot his dear Aunt Berenice has ever done for Junior!"

"Between the two of us it ought to go up pretty quick. It's not going to be any mansion. One floor. One bath. And she won't need a guest room. She hasn't got a friend in the world. Maybe a fireplace to sit by in the evening. Keep her at home and away from here."

Actually he was looking forward with some relief to coming out of retirement, if only temporarily. It had not suited him. He knew of no way to occupy himself except with work.

"You just better not skimp on it if you want to have a minute's peace."

"I'll make it nice. After all, I don't want to shame myself before the neighbors — me a builder by trade, or was — by putting my widowed sister in a shack. Do I?"

"Well, it's going to be a labor of love. If you think you'll ever see a red cent for all your work then, Buster, you're a bigger chump than I take you for."

"Well, like I say, your only sister. Or brother."

"And just who, if I may make so bold, is going to pay for the building materials?"

"Well, I've got a lot of stuff out in the shop left over from my contracting days. Enough of just about everything you need to make a nice little bungalow. It's all just sitting there. Besides, I never paid today's prices for it."

"No, but you could get today's prices for it."

"She'll need what she'll have to live on. Widow-woman."

"Hah! Buy and sell you ten times over. Still got the first dollar she ever laid hands on."

"Well, you know, your parents' daughter."

"Has she ever paid you her share of either of them's funeral expenses? Been diddling you since childhood. Never played a game without cheating. Does it still with Wendell. He's the only person who'll play a game with her. Build her a treehouse. That's where she belongs. In a tree."

Henry enjoyed hearing his wife run down his sister. Berenice might think she had the world fooled but at least one person saw through her.

"Now where are you going to put this house?"

"Over in the northwest corner of the property. As far away from here as possible."

"Just means you'll have that much further to trot to answer her beck and call. You're setting up a sweet life for yourself in your golden years."

At twelve dollars a foot, the well-digger he hired went down two hundred and fifty feet before striking water, for this was a country of floods followed by long dry spells — Dust Bowl country once upon a time. A crew was brought in with a backhoe to sink a septic tank and dig trenches for the leaching field. Then the form was built, the cement mixer summoned and the foundation poured. Junior and he could then set to work. They worked after Junior got off work, into the night, and all day Sundays, holidays.

He wavered between working fast and working slowly. For while he was building a house for his sister he was all the while building a coffin for her husband. He fully expected that upon his announcement of its completion Berenice would say, "Well, Wendell." And Wendell would say, "Yes, Berenice."

What would she do without him? To her he was what a clawing post was to a cat. Henry knew very well what Berenice would do without Wendell. She would turn all her attention upon him.

Now that his stem was wound and he ticking again, he rediscovered all his old skills that he had laid aside. He would need them all. For although he had always been a conscientious craftsman, never before had he worked for a more demanding customer, one harder to satisfy. Like his tools, those skills were a bit dull now and hard to hone, but they were still serviceable. The years of nailing down underlayment, floor boards, shingles, laying tiles had stiffened his knees so that in getting up off them now he almost required a crane, and it was not as easy as it had once been to lift his end of a rafter. His hands that in retirement had shed their lifelong calluses first blistered then regained them. Still, there was pleasure in the curl of a shaving from the plane, pride in the tightness of a joint. To cut a board to measure, fit it in place and drive the nail home was as satisfying as putting a period at the end of a sentence that said just what you wanted said — which, come to think of it, was something he had never done with Berenice.

They worked without plans, which allowed modifications to be made as they went along. Modifications were dictated by one thought: how would this suit Berenice, keep her from complaining — or at least from complaining about everything? He felt her looking over his shoulder every minute. Knowing that it would go unappreciated made it truly a labor of love.

"Right nice little bungalow," he declared when, three months later, it was finished. "If I do say so myself." He spoke without much conviction.

"You'll have to say so yourself," said Junior. "She won't."

The truth of the matter was, it was not finished, for he kept finding fault with it, anticipating Berenice's objections. While waiting for Wendell to pass on to his reward he twice replaced the kitchen cabinet door knobs and drawer pulls. He changed light fixtures. He fussed with this, that and everything. Nice little bungalow, he had called it; in fact, this roomy house, on which he had worked more painstakingly than on any other of his long career, gave him no satisfaction whatever. Viewing it through Berenice's eyes, all he could see in it was all that was wrong with it.

He found difficulty in phrasing his news that the house was ready and waiting for occupancy. It seemed to him that with it he was cutting off his sister's husband's life-support system and hastening her into widowhood. What he did was send her a snapshot of the house. On the back of the snapshot he wrote modestly, "Be it ever so humble."

They came bringing with them all their worldly goods — far too many to fit into the house, spacious as that had grown, for Berenice was one of those people who never threw anything away — in the biggest model of what Susan called a Yawl-Hawl. Berenice was at the wheel of it. Not because Wendell looked weakly but because she never let him drive.

"What did I tell you?" said Susan to Henry. "Never sick a day. Dance on our graves."

"He got better," was Berenice's explanation for Wendell. "Doctor called it a miracle." But her smile was not for Wendell's recovery. It was self-satisfaction in her trickery. Still playing like a cat with her prey, she would later confide, "He can't last long."

At the rate Wendell used up life there was no reason for him not to last forever. He had Berenice to run interference for him. Now he would have his failing health as an excuse to exert himself even less than before. Both would have Henry, and Henry, Jr., to wait on them hand and foot.

"Wendell," said Berenice.

"Yes, Berenice," said Wendell.

"Yonder's your new home. You can see it from here. If you look hard enough. Never mind. It can always be added on to."

# The Apple of
# Discord

I

AN OLD APPLE, a rotten apple, the last one from the bottom of the barrel, shriveled, mottled: that was what his face had come to look like. It was moldy with whiskers now that shaving had become awkward for him, and he sullen and resentful and careless of his appearance. To do it at all after his accident he had had to buy this electric razor. With that clumsy right hand of his he would have peeled himself using a blade. But today was the Big Day, weeks in preparation. Today he was to give away the last of his daughters, and he must put on the best face he could for the occasion, and show that he could be gracious in defeat.

Today's would be the third wedding in the house in as many years. Generations of Bennetts had been married under this roof in apple blossom time, the family tradition. Now after this one there would be no more — never.

Of his three girls the first to leave home was Ellen, the oldest. He had opposed her marriage. He opposed it not only because her intended was not what he wasn't, an orchardman, but also because he was what he was, a preacher. He let his prospective son-in-law know just where he and his boss stood with him.

Who was it who sent His sun and His rain to swell and sweeten and color the fruit on the Bennett trees? He who sent His frost and His hail and His drought and His mold and His bugs to blight and destroy it. *As surely as God made little green apples?* But God didn't make them — *he* did, and God put all His obstacles in his way. He thought of himself with his trees as like one of those welfare mothers abandoned by the father of her children and struggling to raise them on her own. His charges numbered somewhere around ten thousand.

He told the preacher the old story of Farmer Brown. How, after being wiped out repeatedly by all the afflictions of Job, Farmer Brown raised his eyes to heaven and asked, "Dear God, what have I done to deserve this?" "Farmer Brown," said God, "you don't have to 'do' anything. There's just something about you that pisses me off." He himself was surely one of God's chosen, for those whom He loved He scourged and chastened. He was a Bennett, one of the spawn of the original apple vendor. God had borne a grudge against that forbidden fruit ever since Eve.

He paused in his shaving for a moment to think about that ancestress of his. The first woman! The original! What a woman that one must have been! What a prize! In the fall of the mother of them all all would fall. A temptation . . . Furs? Jewels? The lure of a tropical cruise? There where the timeless fashions were the design of the Master and any ornament a detraction from the female form divine? A vacation from Paradise? Another, more attractive man? There was no other man, nor could one ever again be so attractive. Hers was the mold, and castings from it could only approximate the original. Something to tempt her to transgress against her Maker's one prohibition . . .

Something good to eat. Something never before eaten. And so she could not know whether it was good to eat or not. But she could tell just by looking. A thing mouth-watering enough to entice her to disobey the command of the Almighty and risk bringing down upon herself His wrath. There in that Garden of Earthly Delights were all the sweets: pomegranates and peaches and plums, figs, grapes, mangoes — everything to be found in your local supermarket flown in from all over the world, only tree-ripened: cactus pears, pineapples, bananas. But to tempt the original sinner to commit the original sin Satan picked from among the produce the one irresistible one. None of your kiwis nor your passion fruit. And Adam, well aware of what he was up to, and what he was incurring, not even chewing but trying to swallow it down whole. It was for having eaten of the fruit of the tree of the knowledge of good and evil that the first couple were expelled from their garden, before they could find their way to the tree of life everlasting. Well, life everlasting they may have lost by eating that apple, but what fruit, one a day, kept the doctor away? Not prunes, friend.

And now God's latest prank upon His servant Seth: a preacher for a son-in-law.

Ellen revealed a willfulness that he would sooner have expected of either of her sisters. That lifelong docility and dutifulness of hers seemed to have been building up like water behind a dam. It now burst. It almost made him change his mind about her and press his opposition to the marriage harder. Perhaps she had in her more of the grit of which farmwives were made than he had given her credit for. But orchardmen were getting scarce hereabouts. It was unrealistic of him to hope any longer to find one for all three girls. Let Ellen have her preacher. The blessing he gave her was grudging, but he gave it. Write her off as the wild card in the deck; he had two more to deal.

He lowered the razor and peered at his face in the mirror searching in vain for a likeness between himself and his offspring. Those stepdaughters of Eve, his daughters, they none of them cared for apples. Bennetts — and they didn't care for apples! Doris, the "in-between one," as she called herself, wouldn't touch one. Said she knew too well what work and worry had gone into it. Said that for her the sight of her poor mother, her old knees ruined long ago from kneeling to sort them, put a worm in each and every one. As for him, well, never mind how old he was but he was old — people told him so to his face: "I can't blame you for selling out. You've got nobody to leave the place to and you'll soon be too old to work it yourself anymore." He had attained his age by eating apples enough each day to keep three doctors away.

Who were those girls of his to say they didn't want to be apple farmers? Neither had he "wanted" to be one. He was *born* one. He did not choose, he was chosen. He had not asked to be left-handed, green-eyed, red-headed either, but so he was. He had cut his teeth on apples. That was what it was to be a Bennett!

He had put all three through college. He was not one of those who thought that higher education was not for women; on the contrary, he thought it was for women only — men were meant for practical affairs. How had he paid for their tuition? With McIntoshes, Cortlands, Macouns, Red Delicious, Greenings: so many crates per credit-hour. The fruit of knowledge. Apples for the teacher. The best schooling. Vassar College! The mistake of his life. How you gonna keep 'em down on the farm after they've seen Poughkeepsie?

Why had the farmboys he exposed them to all been so backward? No boldness, no spunk in any of them. To get that dowry of ten thousand trees, bridal-like with blossoms in the spring, aglow with fruit in the fall, he would have seduced one of the farmer's daughters, any one, hoping that she got caught and he be marched to the altar by her old man with a shotgun at his back, chortling to himself all the way up the aisle.

Certainly none of those boys could have held back out of fear that the girl's father found him unacceptable on closer inspection. He was prepared to overlook shortcomings. He encouraged them. He bucked them up when their hopes flagged. He kept them going by misleading them about their prospects. In fact, certain shortcomings he was looking for in his sons-in-law. It was doubly frustrating because the very backwardness — sometimes the none-too-brightness — that kept them from putting themselves forward was the attribute he sought. Broad backs and brawny arms were what they were to furnish — his girls would supply the brains. He wanted his daughters to wear the pants in their families. He wanted them to twist their husbands around their little fingers.

His stock of daughters dwindling, he opposed Doris's marriage more vigorously by far than he had opposed Ellen's. Another non-farmer. An undertaker — "mortician" he preferred to be called. Somebody had to do it, of course. Nothing more essential. But what more thankless a job was there? How could she sleep at night knowing what thing lay on that marble slab in the basement workshop? How could she tolerate the touch of those hands of his knowing what they had been busy at earlier in the day? How could you raise your children in a charnel house, and how did other children look on yours? How could you bear to be always in the hush of mourning among grieving survivors dressed in black? Why not a doctor instead, somebody whose business it was to keep people alive? Or better still, an apple farmer, one whose job it was to keep the doctor away.

So with two down and only one to go, he now had for sons-in-law one to put him under and another to get him a pass to that nursing home in the sky where you play bingo in eternity.

The pair of them often teamed up on the same case. This thought would in time put into his mind a scheme. A way of ensuring that his third and last son-in-law be the orchardman he wanted. More specifically, Pete Jeffers, a man like himself, with cider, hard cider, in his veins.

One man's misfortune is another man's fortune. He had sometimes been the beneficiary of that one-sided exchange, though always mindful that it might just as easily have been the other way round. Apple farming had its rewards but it was a risky business. It could drive you to desperation. It could drive you crazy.

Some years ago a neighbor of his caught a woman in his orchard threshing one of the trees. He was a worried man. Crops had been poor for years and this one promised to be no better. He was deeply in debt. The chronic shortage of pickers had forced him into the pick-your-own business, something no farmer liked because in picking the apples inexperienced pickers broke off the buds of many of next year's apples. Now the man went berserk. He grabbed the woman's stick from her and threshed her with it. She died from a blow to her head. He spent the rest of his life in the state asylum for the criminally insane. The farm his family was forced to sell became part of Seth Bennett's.

Of all the natural enemies of orchardmen the two most dreaded were a late spring frost when the trees were in blossom and a summer hailstorm when the fruit was on them. You could spray against insects and fungus, you could poison the mice that girdled the trees and the woodchucks that burrowed beneath their roots, shoot the deer, but against frost and hail you were helpless. If the fruit was not destroyed by the hail it was pocked, unappetizing-looking, unmarketable except to the baby-food processors, for a portion of the price it would have fetched. That insurance against it was available was a bad joke; nobody could afford the premium.

After losing his wife to cancer, then being wiped out by hail two years in a row, Seth Bennett's neighbor Tom Jeffers went out in his ruined orchard and put a bullet in his heart. He left his only child Pete to sell out to developers and pay off his debts. Pete had lived at home, his father's partner.

Seth Bennett felt beholden to Pete Jeffers as a combat veteran might have felt toward the orphan of a buddy who had taken the bullets meant for them both. For although their two farms were little more than a mile apart, such was the capriciousness of hail that his had been spared both times by the storms that struck Tom Jeffers' twice.

Of late, on nights when the trees had to be sprayed, it was Janet, home from school now, who drove the tractor that pulled him on the sprayer. She would not allow her mother, with those knees of hers, to spend the night out in the chill and the damp.

Now that the two older girls were gone from home their rooms were unused. Pete Jeffers was homeless. Pete knew apples. Molly was old. So, for that matter, was he. He could use a helper, an experienced hand. Pete was a fine fellow. Quiet, serious-minded, with a farmer's patience and tenacity. Pete was unmarried. He was just three years older than Janet.

To the sign on the road that read, "Garden of Eden Orchards. Pick Your Own. Seth Bennett, Prop." was now added, "Peter Jeffers, Manager."

"I want you to think of us as your family, Pete," he said.

Including Janet, he added to himself. But not as your sister.

What a workhorse the man turned out to be! Never still. Busy every minute of the day. Handy at everything, not just at the daily farm duties. Fixed, patched, mended, repaired, painted, cleaned, straightened — things needing doing for years. Even on Sundays. So eager to be doing he had no time for talk at table, was up and out while still chewing. This during the off-season. The time came to gear up for the year's crop. What that young fellow didn't know about apple farming wasn't worth knowing. Born to it, in it all his life, had it in his blood. What a treasure he would be when he took over the place!

Trouble was, you couldn't get him to slow down long enough to spend any time together with Janet. Was there another woman in his life? That would be a sorry repayment for the hospitality he had been shown as a homeless orphan! But no, there could be no other woman: he never left the place, never took a minute off much less a night out. His would-be father-in-law began to wonder whether Pete was not one of those born bachelors, living only to work. He seemed to have no pleasures, no personal life. Busying himself to keep his mind off his parents, said Seth to himself, and waited for Pete to come out of his mourning and take note of the world around him.

Meanwhile, to hasten that process he threw the two of them together whenever possible — and groaned inwardly at Pete's backwardness as he spied on them. "Molly's knees are bad this evening," he would say, giving her a look, after dinner. "Pete, be a good boy and dry the dishes for Janet." Pete did, and that was all he did: dry dishes. The evening still young, he would excuse himself, and Molly, for bed, and he was scarcely out of his recliner before Pete was out of his armchair, saying good-night to all. Her father bought Janet a car, her first, and Pete taught her to drive. Seated that close, on back country roads, lovers' lanes . . . Janet passed her license test on her first try.

"Pete," he said, "let's you and me have a talk. Father to son. I think of you as my adopted son. Who knows? — maybe one day soon we will be closer than that. My hope is that we will.

"As you know, I've got no son of my own to leave the farm to. What I have got is one daughter still unmarried. As far as I'm concerned, she's yours if you want her."

"But she doesn't like me."

"What are you saying! Of course she likes you."

"I don't mean she *dislikes* me. But she doesn't *like* me."

"Don't I know her? Do I know this old palm of mine? My own daughter? I know her better than she knows herself. I tell you she likes you."

"Then she certainly doesn't show it."

"You don't understand women. They're supposed to play hard to get. Would you want one who threw herself at you? You appreciate them more if you have to overcome some resistance. They're clever creatures and they know that. They're like horses: they have to be broken. They shy from you at first and dash all over the lot, but their curiosity about you is aroused and in time they come to your whistle and nuzzle you as you slip the halter over their heads. To wear them down you have to keep after them. They'll buck and throw you when you first try to mount them but they accept your weight after a while. Well, I took that a little further than I meant to, but my point is made. Keep after her, boy. Faint heart never won fair lady. Maybe you don't like her enough?"

"Oh, yes, I do. She's attractive. She's bright. Educated. Has an agreeable disposition. Everything a man could want in a wife."

"And with her comes the farm. Ten thousand trees! Three hundred and twenty acres! A kingdom all your own! And more than that: Molly and me. You have to think of that, too. Sometimes, you know, in-laws don't get along so well — especially when they live under the same roof. In fact, there are people who, although they want their daughter to marry, resent the man who takes her from them. That's contrary; still, it's human nature for you. But we would welcome you into the family. You have my blessing. And I can speak for Molly, too. Now it's up to you, son. She's just waiting for you to make known your intentions. Take my word."

One variety of apple, just one, the Cortland, consistently twinned: two stems from a common bud, the identical fruit hanging cheek by cheek. He and his Janet were a pair of Cortlands. Neither of them could think a thought without the other knowing it. She would understand what was expected of her now. Her sisters having married to their father's disappointment, it was up to her to put things right. Child of her parents' old age, plainly the last, she had been petted by all the family, given her own way in everything. She was deeply in their debt. The time had come for her to discharge that debt.

"Well, Janet, I suppose you'll be thinking of getting married before long now." Her sister Doris's wedding was barely over before he said that to her.

"I'm not in any hurry," she said.

But he was. He was still a long way from the finish line, but his face as he shaved every morning (this was before he broke his left arm) told him that he was in the home stretch. Janet must be spurred.

The tombstone cutter he went to was the son, maybe the grandson, of the one with whom he had last dealt. That occasion was the burial of his mother. The Bennetts were a long-lived clan. In their old family graveyard on the farm lay many who had lasted into their nineties. And that was before the miracles of modern medicine. An apple a day . . .

The stonecutter was putting the finishing touches to a job; be right with him. He wore goggles and over his nose and mouth a mask. Through a rubber stencil glued to the face of the stone he was carving the last digit in the date of some person's death. He did it not with a hammer and chisel but with a jet of fine metal pellets propelled by an airbrush like the charge of a shotgun. To protect himself from their rebound he wore a blacksmith's leather apron. He now finished his job, pushed up his goggles and pulled down his mask, peeled off the stencil, ran his forefinger over the engraving and gave a nod of approval.

When he learned that the stone his customer wanted to order was one for himself and his wife the mason commended his good sense and his consideration for his heirs. It was so right and yet so rare. Knowing his true motive, and protected by his heritage of longevity, he enjoyed the man's misplaced admiration for what he took to be his foresight.

"I can't think of a more important decision for people to make for themselves, nor one more personal. Yet most of them can't bring themselves to do it. And that's foolish because, let's face it, the time is coming — which of us knows when? — and the sensible thing is to do it while you can, the way *you* want it done, not leave it to your survivors. I've seen them here almost come to blows over what Mom or Pop would have liked. Children all have different notions one from another about their parents, and nothing brings it out like that last decision. In the end, with the best intentions in the world, they may choose something you wouldn't think suitable for you at all, and whatever it is you're the one who's going to have to live with it, so to speak, 'in perpetuity,' as we say."

They were now outdoors where the firm's wares were displayed, a selection of stones, clean-faced, innocent of inscription, like an orphanage standing at inspection for a choice of adoption and the bestowal of a name.

"What I want is simple," he said. "A single stone for my wife and myself. Here. I've written it down. It's to read, 'Seth. Molly.' Underneath each name the years of birth and death. Then this epitaph: 'Comfort me with apples . . .'"

"With, of course, the family name. I mention that because we charge by the letter."

"That won't be necessary. Anyone who sees it will know."

"Well, I'll put your information, your vital statistics, as we say, on file, and the stone will be carved and put in place after the burial of whichever of you survives the other."

"I'd like to have it in place by this time next week."

"While both of you are still alive?"

"That's why I'm buying it now."

"Burial is difficult when the stone is already in place. The backhoe disturbs it."

"In this case there will be little disturbance. We're going to be cremated."

They would have been even if the modern sanitary code had not prescribed it in cases of burial in private family graveyards. He had no intention of spending his last night aboveground on that marble slab in his son-in-law's basement.

"Is it to go in the Protestant cemetery or the Catholic?"

"Neither."

The family graveyard lay out of sight of the house at a distance from it of a hundred yards. In it were buried three generations of Bennetts — with space remaining for several more, descendants to come of that son-in-law, the orchardman, whom he was bent on having. All his life long he had laid flowers on those graves, had mowed and weeded and raked among them, had straightened their headstones after the heavings of the frost. He had lived to an age that made even those of his dead whom he remembered remote in time from him. Of the others he had forgotten just what the kinship to him of many of them was.

But the knowledge was comforting that all were his, Bennetts by birth or grafted onto the stock, tenants of his domain. Comforting, too, was the old-fashioned quaintness of their headstones: weather-worn, mossy tablets of white marble, some with inscriptions so effaced by time and the elements as to be nearly indecipherable, others with their stilted epitaphs and archaic spelling, they made death seem like something that used to happen to people.

The transaction was concluded with, "Mr. Bennett, sir, we appreciate your patronage, and" pointing with his pencil first to the blank space following the year of Seth's birth, and the dash following that, then to Molly's, "may it be a long time before I'm called on to fill in those."

He could not resist saying, "Hold on, young fellow. When that time comes you may not be here yourself."

"How well I know! But if I'm not somebody will be."

The mason and his crew with their crane and backhoe arrived on the worksite after Janet went off to her job in the morning and were finished and gone by the time she got home in the evening. Thus she never knew the stone was there until he showed it to her.

He was pleased with his production. The setting: soil sacred to her family, its shrine, its collective crypt. The cast: all her ancestors, born here, buried here, an unbroken line of succession, inheritance. She could not but feel their eloquent silence, their call, their claim on her. Each marble marker was the tablet of the law, proclaiming her identity, her duty. And now this latest one, her parents', with its impending dates, its Biblical injunction, passed on the torch to her. From out of the corner of his eye he slyly studied its effect.

It was quick in coming.

"Oh, Father!" she cried, and burst into tears.

She had never called him "Father" before, always "Papa," and the unaccustomed name distanced him from himself, made him feel as though he was being spoken of in the third person, posthumously.

She flung herself, sobbing, into his arms.

Shaken, shamed, he said, patting her back, "Now, now. I'm not under there yet," although he could almost feel the weight upon him of that granite block, which stared at him over her heaving shoulder. It now seemed to him the worst of bad jokes at his own expense, and there it would sit to mock him with that blank space waiting to be filled in. "It's just the sensible thing to do. Not leave it to you and your sisters. The three of you might not agree on what we would have wanted."

She was supposed to have said that she would carry on her parents' lives, marry Pete and keep the farm in the family. If not on the spot then soon afterwards. She did neither, despite her father's urging Pete to "strike while the iron is hot." If she noticed them at all, she found Pete's timid attentions out of place at a time when she was saddened by the prospect of her parents' deaths.

With the elasticity of youth, Janet recovered from the scare he had given her, and she cheered him by pointing out to him how long-lived their family was. So, while encouraging Pete in his slow suit, he plotted to help him with a different tack, a more immediate threat, a further variation upon the theme of "it's later than you think." Confident of winning, he was enjoying this game he and Janet were playing. He was pleased with himself and with her. She was calling his bluff. That baby girl of his, she was his match — almost.

The nearby town could expand in just three directions, for it was bounded on the west by the Hudson River. It was spreading rapidly as commuting distance to New York extended ever northward. The Hudson was tidal, and a tide of workers now flowed with it down to the city in the morning and back up in the evening. The local acreage was becoming too valuable to farm, the inducement to the natives to parcel and sell theirs too tempting to withstand. Dairy herds had been auctioned off, orchards uprooted, pastures paved over. What had been a land of milk and honey (bees were the orchardman's best friends: they pollinated his blossoms) had been converted into shopping plazas and developments. Now it was like a game of Monopoly, houses on every square. In all the area the old Bennett place was the largest tract remaining in agriculture, and the neighbors wanted it kept that way. It had taken on a status somewhat akin to a preserve, a park, a public trust.

To get a permit to subdivide and develop his land application must be made to the village planning board for a variance in the zoning code. A public hearing would be held. It would be reported in the local paper. There was little doubt that he would get his permit; he could hardly be denied what so many had been granted. But just because so many had, and so few places remained unspoiled, there would be opposition. It would come mostly from the city people, recent transplants, keen on keeping things as they were. This he expected, but he was not prepared for the volume. On the night of the meeting there was such a turnout that the nearest parking place to the village hall he could find was three blocks away. Good! Let Janet see how widespread was the opposition to the move she was forcing him to consider.

He was not obliged to be present at the hearing. He wanted to be, to enjoy the hostility he had stirred up. He entered the hall feeling as unpopular as an out-of-town fighter about to enter the ring with the local champion. In the community where he was the fourth generation of his family he had become an outcast. What none of these people knew was that he had no intention of doing what he was there to get permission to do. On the contrary. Getting the permission was his way of keeping it from happening.

The concerns expressed by the citizens interested were civic-minded, concerns for the common good. They worried about the additional tax burden for schools and teachers and buses on the elderly, the pensionnaires, the young couples just starting out and having a hard enough time already making ends meet. They feared for the safety of children on the busier roads. Those roads would have to be patrolled more, perhaps widened as well, would certainly require more upkeep, and all that too would mean higher taxes for those least able to afford them. The county landfill was already full to overflowing. There was the threat to the purity of the aquifer with so many more septic systems. The added strain on the volunteer fire department, the rescue squad, the already overcrowded county hospital. Tourism would suffer from the reduction in the deer herd, still one of the area's attractions. Hotel keepers, restaurant owners, sporting goods stores, filling stations, all would feel the pinch if the trend represented by this application for a variance in the zoning code were allowed to continue unchecked. A line must be drawn somewhere.

One person present took these community concerns and alarms seriously. He. Those who mouthed them were concerned for one thing: their pocketbooks, the devaluation of their properties. He didn't blame them. He took it seriously too. If only they knew that he was their masked champion, fighting their fight! Let them raise every objection — the heavier the burden on Janet's conscience. The courtship of that latter-day

John Alden, Pete Jeffers, was being won for him in a town meeting, not by a denial of his future father-in-law's petition to break up the family farm but by the granting of it. A weapon like a plastic pistol: harmless but scary-looking.

Throughout the meeting he sat silent. He could not take the floor and say, "I agree with everything you've said. Tell it to that daughter of mine."

However, not all were against him that evening. There were two factions. Those against him, by far the more numerous of the two, were the ones who were there by virtue of other farmers' having done what he was asking permission to do, subdivide and develop his land. These were the city people. They *had been* city people and to the natives they always *would be* city people. A stranger could have distinguished one side from the other on sight. The city people dressed country casual, the country folks in their city best for the occasion. The city people had moved to the country to escape the city. Now they were like immigrants who passed anti-immigration laws to keep out more like themselves. These new locals would have erected, running about down the middle of Poughkeepsie, a Berlin Wall if they could.

Those for him were the few remaining holdout farmers. The newcomers wanted to legislate that they go on being farmers and thus preserve for them the charm and tranquillity of the countryside. The farmers didn't give a damn about the charm and tranquillity of the countryside. They wanted to go on being farmers, although it got harder all the time, and the reason it did was the steady invasion of these outsiders driving up the cost of everything, but be damned if they were going to be told what they could and could not do with their property by a bunch of Johnny-come-latelies from downstate.

After a period of delay sufficiently long to make it look as if consideration had been given to the opposition before a decision was reached, his application for a zoning variance was approved by the village planning board. Now Janet would come to her senses, marry Pete, and keep the farm in the family. It was not that he disbelieved in the power of love, or the power of the absence of it, it was rather that he could not understand how it could prevail over ten thousand apple trees and three hundred and twenty acres of land that had been her family's for four generations, she the fifth.

"All right," said the real estate agent, humoring the old fellow. "If you insist we'll list it first as a farm. I can see how for sentimental reasons you might want to try to keep it intact. Been in the family for generations and all that. But it's a good thing you've got that zoning variance up your sleeve because you know as well as I do what's happening to farm acreage in this area."

He winced, as he always did, at the expression "farm acreage." It made land seem like something divisible into small parcels.

"And the young people don't want to farm anymore."

"My boy Pete here does."

"Then he's one of a kind."

"You can say that again!"

"Has Pete got the wherewithal to buy you out? Like I say, we'll offer it for a while as a farm. But, believe me, a developer is the only buyer you're going to find — and you'll have no trouble finding one of those. They've all had their eye on this property for years. Even had aerial photographs taken of it. Prime building land. Highly desirable homesites. Got a view of the Catskills from any plot on the place, once it's cleared. I've had several ask me to approach you with an offer, and they've gone up with each and every one. You can cry all the way to the bank."

It was just what he wanted to hear. Or wanted Janet to hear. Which was why he had invited the agent to stay for supper, unless his wife was expecting him. He was not married. "And afterwards," the man said, "you can move down to Florida and lie in the sun all day long. No more spraying bugs through the night. No more worries over the weather. You've earned your rest."

"I don't speak Spanish," he said. "Or Yiddish."

Janet refilled their guest's plate. He had a bachelor's appreciation of good home cooking, and he had walked up a hearty appetite today. She had shown him over the property, at her father's request. The place had been surveyed, by link and chain, some 200 years ago. That had always been good enough, until now. Never in all that while had there been a dispute over the lines between the Bennetts and any of their adjoining neighbors. Having Janet pace off the boundaries would bring home to her as nothing else had the threat of losing it. Now the man attacked his second helpings no less enthusiastically than the first. But the elder Bennetts and Pete pushed away their unfinished plates.

Apples. First crop we had a record of. And that pioneer farm family lost heavily on it. They too were forced from their orchard. In apple farming you won a round now and then but you lost as many or more. Why do it then? Why play the game with the deck stacked against you? For the satisfaction of taking on a sure-fire winner, nothing less than nature herself, the elements. Brought out the grit in you. A contest worthy of a man. Coming off second best was not bad when your opponent was the unbeatable all-time champ. If they'd had it to do over again Adam and Eve would have done it. Apple farmers were like that. Born, not made. You inherited it. Maybe through a strain from that original couple. And because your forebears had endured its hardships for your sake you owed it to them to endure what they had endured. They expected that of you, no less. What was it that kept us from flying off into outer space? And how was that discovered? Ah, if only an apple would fall on Janet's head, teach her the law of gravity, and tie her down to her native soil!

It mystified him how, his blood fueling her, she could tramp over the property with the real estate dealer and every prospective buyer he brought out and not comprehend what a prize she was letting go. By now the agent could have shown the place himself, so many times had they gone together over it, but she insisted on accompanying every party. Offers were made but on the agent's advice, or so he pretended, he was accepting none because they kept going up all the time. Yet even this did not increase the worth of her property to Janet. It did to him. It made it all the harder to sell.

"You realize, Pete," he said across the breakfast table one morning during this period, "that with the disappearance of orchards hereabouts, combined with the increase in population, which is to say the market, the price of locally grown apples is sure to soar. Instead of succumbing to offers to sell, now is the time for farmers to hold on. I know it's what I would do if only I were younger, or had somebody to carry on after me. This place is going to be a gold mine, with somebody in charge who knows the business. The day will come when apples are individually wrapped in foil like chocolates. I may not live to see it, but it can't be far off.

"So now, what are we going to be doing today? You're the manager."

"More of the same. Planting trees."

"Planting trees!" said Molly to Janet. "If those two don't take the cake. The place is up for sale, and they're still planting trees."

"This building boom we're in is a bubble that could go bust overnight. Overnight. Then what's left? Farmland. Got you a place with no mortgage to foreclose — and this has never had one since the dawn of Creation — you won't be selling apples on streetcorners. You'll be supplying them."

"Planting trees. At your age."

"We orchardmen take the long view. Eh, Pete? Father to son. Or son-in-law, as the case may be. As long as this remains an orchard it's going to be treated as one. That means replacing trees. Maybe one of my grandchildren will want to farm it."

"You haven't got any grandchildren. And if you were to have one tomorrow it would come of working age about the time these trees you're planting bear their first fruit. You expect to live to see that?"

"I expect to be feeding people long after I'm dead. When you think, Pete, of the work that goes into an orchard! The work and the faith. Your grandfather planted that tree, your father that one. They did it for their children, we do it for ours. Can you just imagine the heartbreak of seeing them all torn up by the roots?"

"I don't have to imagine it. I have seen it done."

"I'm sorry I mentioned it, son. That was thoughtless of me."

An offer was made by a developer which the agent advised him to accept. He did. He accepted it with no intention of living up to the agreement but in order to impress Janet with his determination, with the worth of her patrimony and her duty to preserve it. For the announcement of his acceptance the agent was invited to supper. He felt not one twinge of conscience over using and misleading the fellow. He did not like him, nor any of his breed. Merchants of misery, of broken homes, deaths, ruination, old age, spoliation. Besides, he had practically boarded him.

"Looks like I've got no choice but to take it," he sighed.

Never was so much money accepted so ungratefully. It was an awesome sum. It made him realize as never before what he would be sacrificing. The amount shocked him, shamed him, made him feel a bigger culprit, contemptible in the eyes of all the living and of all his ancestors now turning over in their graves out behind the house. He listened with one ear to the offer while listening with the other one for Janet's voice relenting at the eleventh hour.

She was calling his bluff, forcing him to show every card in his hand. He had now played all but the last one: the closing. Meanwhile, nothing had been signed, all was still pending. Backing out of the deal even after a binder had been put down was a common occurrence. He would gladly refund a buyer's binder.

He could no longer rely upon that telepathy he had believed to exist between him and her. She was younger than he realized, childish, less sensitive, less dutiful. Truth was, her mother and her sisters had spoiled her. People used to do the things expected of them out of a sense of obligation, but today's youth — irresponsible, selfish. It was time for a showdown. He would be tactful, fatherly — all that; but he would be firm, and he would have his way.

"Listen here, Janet," he said. "It's time you and I had a talk."

She agreed, for she had something to say to him.

"*You've* got something to say to *me?* What is it?"

"I'm engaged. Engaged to be married. You've got all your daughters off your hands now. Well, aren't you going to congratulate me?"

"Who is he?" he demanded.

"Rod."

"Rod? Rod who?"

"Why, Rodney Evans, of course. What other Rod do we know?"

He did not know any Rodney Evans. Who the hell was Rodney Evans? There could be no Rodney Evans, for none figured in his plans. Then he knew who Rodney Evans was. He had been a part of his plans but this was not the part he was cast for. Rodney Evans was not a person, he was the real estate agent — him with hair like a meringue — meant to scare her with. Rodney Evans was the serpent he himself had invited into his garden. Pete Jeffers had lived under the same roof with her for nine months and never gotten to first base; this Rodney Evans had begun his successful suit on their initial walk together over the property.

"It was love at first sight," she said.

"Shame on you, Father! Trying to make your daughter marry a man she does not love."

"But you *will* love him. You will. In time. Pete will make you the best of husbands. You've seen him up close. You know how he lives. Hard-working. Easygoing. Good-natured. Home-loving. Thrifty. Dependable. Has no bad habits. Doesn't drink — or only a drop now and then. Doesn't go out to bars. Doesn't go out *anywhere*. Doesn't gamble. Doesn't chase after women. Why, I've never even heard him curse! And there's another thing. (This is just between you and me.) There's a lot to be said for being brighter than your husband. You're not just better educated but a lot brighter than Pete, and he knows it. He would look up to you. You can twist him around your little finger. And I know you. You're like me. You like having your own way in everything. Eh? And why not! Well, with him you would."

"Father, you are becoming more shameful by the moment. You're proposing a husband for your daughter on the grounds that he's not too bright. And he's supposed to be a friend of yours!"

"Listen. Marry Pete and I'll leave everything to you. Everything. Your sisters don't need it. Their husbands have got the most secure jobs in the world. People are going to go on dying and trying to get to heaven for the foreseeable future."

"Father! I will not be a party to robbing my sisters of their inheritance."

"You always were my favorite. You know that."

A silence fell. Between father and daughter passed a perception. It was as though he were wooing her for himself.

"I know nothing of the sort. And I don't want to hear it. How can I face my sisters? If I'm your favorite now it's because I'm the one still unmarried. Do you realize what you are doing and what it makes you? You are tempting me with the apple."

"Millions of them! Millions! Tell me, what have you got against Pete?"

"Nothing. I've got nothing against Pete. I like him. But I don't love him. He's supposed to be a friend of yours. Would you want your friend to marry a woman who didn't love him? I like Pete too much to wish that on him. What is more, I have no reason to think he loves me. Or anybody else, for that matter. Pete doesn't know what love is."

"He respects you."

"Once and for all, Father, I will never marry a man I do not love. Did you have me only so I could carry on this farm?"

"It's been in our family, yours and mine, for four generations."

"That's long enough. Time for a change."

"That does it! Now you listen to your father, young lady."

"Listen to your daughter, old man. You are forgetting that you are my father."

"Marry Pete, and everything will be yours. Marry this what's-his-name —"

"Rodney. Rodney Evans. And I will soon be Mrs. Rodney Evans."

"— and I will leave everything to be divided between your sisters."

"You're no father, you're ... you're a breeder. A stock-breeder."

He fell silent, struck by a truth in what she had said. A twist to it of which she herself was unaware, and the difference in their outlooks made him feel the difference in their ages, the gap between the generations, made him feel that indeed he was not the father of his children — or rather, that they were not the children of their father. Yes, he had "bred" them with a career for them in mind, as he had been bred. He had given them life, that was to say, he had passed on to them the life passed on to him. He had housed them, fed them, clothed them, educated them, nursed them. Yet it was not he alone who had done that. He had been a link in the chain. Fruit from trees set out by their grandparents had paid their bills. Did they owe nothing to those who had worked and worried and denied themselves and put aside for their unborn offspring? Were they now free to do just as they pleased, mate to their fancy, outside the strain, without consideration for their forebears? He had expected that their long-lineaged genes would shape and guide them. They thought the world began with themselves. For him the world was ending with himself.

"Father," she said, in a different, a reflective tone, "you ought to have traveled. Seen something of the world. Then you wouldn't think that the sun rises and sets over this farm of yours."

How he hated it when people, especially young whipper-snappers, told him what he should do or should have done!

"To have one spot of earth that is all the world to him — that is what I call a fortunate man. That it costs him work and worry now and then makes it all the dearer."

"What reward has it brought you?"

"Independence! I have been my own man."

"Independence! You've been a slave. Ten thousand masters you've got. You belong to those trees. They don't even let you sleep."

It was always hard work; chainsaws and tractors made it dangerous work. Throughout the growing season you were often out on the sprayer all night long, and the chemicals were hazardous to your health: to your lungs, your eyes, your skin. When it came to spraying you were damned if you did and damned if you didn't. The insects and the fungi could blight and canker your fruit, but the chemicals that poisoned them also poisoned the birds that ate them. Worse by far, the chemicals killed the bees upon which your whole operation depended, without which your blossoms went unpollinated. It was not like that in the original Garden of Eden. Those gates at which the flaming sword would be set kept out the bugs. The Hudson Valley lay east of Eden — though in the spring you would have thought it was Paradise regained.

There was no season of rest. Harvest-time did not bring months by the fireside in your carpet slippers. Pruning — a never-ending job — was done in the depth of winter, mowing at the height of summer; you shivered and you sweltered. The trees of each variety ripened separately; you were at it sixteen hours a day. The apples must be sorted, graded, packed, shipped. The "drops" must be gathered from the ground and sent to the cider mill. You might find that before you had time to wrap the trunks to protect them, the deer had eaten the bark of your saplings and killed them. Five minutes of hail or six months of drought — hard to say which was the longer to live through — and your crop was gone.

But with the pickers in the trees singing like birds — if birds could warble words — and shouting jokes to one another, and with that red river of ripe fruit flowing along the conveyor belt — was it *you* who grew all that? Construction workers on skyscraper girders, tugboat crews, road-menders, assembly-line workers, schoolchildren from here to California would polish off lunch with one of your apples.

Meanwhile, sure, like farmers everywhere, he pore-mouthed. Once when he was inveighing against his hardships one of those sons-in-law of his commiserated with him by saying he couldn't understand why anybody in his right mind would go in for it.

"You're not in your right mind!" he said proudly. "You don't 'go in for' it. You're born to it. It's in your blood."

His worst year was to have been his best. The weather was balmy. With the warming of the days, like popcorn in a pan, first a few blossoms, then more, then in a burst the trees whitened. The air was drowsy with the buzz of bees. Though the days were warm, the nights were cool: the prescription for growing. The rain was regulated as though by the Department of Agriculture. He was encouraged by these conditions to work harder than he had ever worked before. The trees sagged with fruit. Incandescent as Christmas trees they were in the glow of the setting sun when he went out to inspect his ripening crop. Money didn't grow on trees? Who said? When they were apple trees it did! It almost restored his long-lost faith, at least for a season. God was in His heaven and all was right with the world, quoted Ellen, the Vassar College English major who would in time marry the mealy-mouthed minister. He suspected that God was out of His heaven, leaving some sleepy subordinate to mind the store. Only then would orchardmen have such luck.

The days when school was let out and whole families came to pick apples, bringing a picnic lunch with them (he supplied the iced tubs of beer and soda) were a thing of the past. Now labor contractors went to Florida, Jamaica, the Bahamas and signed up migrant gangs. The farmer housed them in trailer camps or in area motels. They chattered incessantly as they worked. Listening to them was like getting hard of hearing: it was English they were speaking, you knew it was, yet you could not make out the words. But it was musical. They were as noisy in the trees as nesting wrens and just as merry. Last year his pickers had been Jamaicans and so they would be again this year.

The fruit was almost ripe for picking when the state legislature, under pressure from labor unions, passed a measure requiring aliens to obtain work permits, and making it impossible for them to do so.

He watched his finest crop go unpicked, fall to the ground and rot.

"What do you think — life is a picnic?" he said. "Think I would sooner have had it soft? Sit in a bank making loans to people? Sell their houses out from under them? Brokers in heartbreak! I've fed people. And more than that. Not just staple food. Joyful food. What children love to steal. There's satisfaction in that. No, it hasn't always been easy. But man must eat his bread in the sweat of his face."

"Father, remember how that curse came upon us?"

*Going once.*

*Going twice.*

He was like an auctioneer egging on two competing bidders. Except that one, Janet, was not competing.

*Going . . .*

*Going . . .*

*Gone!*

It was the commission he would earn on the sale of the Bennett farm that put Rodney Evans in a position to propose marriage. So, with a sense of the fitness of it which he expected him to share, he informed his future father-in-law. This commission was staying in the family.

The terms of the sale left them with a lifehold on the house and five acres right around it. At once, even before the clearing of it began, his former land, the land of his family, was like a lake surrounding his little island. Just so he felt himself cut off from his neighbors, his former friends. The very trees, now awaiting execution, the trees whose pruning he had overseen as watchfully as a mother the barbering of her brood, reproached him for his treachery — or would have if he had ventured among them.

On the morning a week after the closing they were awakened by noises as if war had broken out all around them: bursts of machine-gun fire, the rumble of tanks. Although expected, it still came as a shock, and they clung to each other, frightened by this upheaval in their lives. The temptation was to pull the covers over their heads and stay in bed, but drawn by a contrary curiosity he dressed and went outdoors.

Men with chainsaws were in the trees as pruners had once been, only these were not just trimming out the unwanted suckers, they were lopping off all the limbs. Above one pile hovered a pair of songbirds protesting the destruction of their nest with its eggs. Already half a dozen trees had been topped, leaving a row of stumps three feet tall.

Now the bulldozer was brought on. It lumbered up to a stump, lowering its blade like a buck his antlers to engage a rival. For a minute the contest was a stand-off. The tree resisted, clung to its hold. Then as though in mounting rage the engine growled deeper and deeper as the operator summoned up its lowermost gears. Its treads dug into the ground. The tree yielded, toppled, its roots tore loose and surfaced. One after another the stumps were attacked. Then they and their limbs were pushed into a pile. The holes left looked like bomb craters. The pile was doused with kerosene and set afire. Being green, the wood smoked thickly. Soon the scene was like one of those days when fog from off the River blanketed the Valley.

It was not that he had never before seen an apple tree uprooted, even whole sections of the orchard. Space was valuable, spray and fertilizer expensive, and when trees became old and unproductive they had to be culled out. But they were replaced with young stock.

And so, although their working days were over and they might have slept late now, they were up as early as before, awakened by the roar of the bulldozers and the snarl of the chainsaws on all sides of them. It was as though they were surrounded by packs of lions and tigers prowling from dawn to dusk.

Up and down the roads all around he went on his motorcycle, calling on his neighbors. His message to them was, "I tried to sell it as a going farm, keep it together like it's always been. It was advertised that way in the paper for months, and that paper is read the length and breadth of the Valley. The real estate agent shared the listing with other agents in six counties. My family has farmed it for four generations and I was ready to sell it for a lot less if only it could be kept intact. Not an offer did I get. Not a prospect. I don't know what the world is coming to when nobody wants to farm anymore.

"I never expected it would come to this. I expected my daughters to marry farmers and carry on as always before. Out of three, one at least one would. But those girls of mine all fell far from the tree. How it hurts me to have to say that!

"Put yourself in my place. I planted those trees. I fertilized them. I protected them against their enemies. Whenever the radio warned of an invasion of insects or mold, I was up with them all night like a father with a sick child. Only I had ten thousand children to nurse. To see them being uprooted breaks my old heart."

*You can cry all the way to the bank:* those who did not say that to his face looked it.

"Believe me, it's not the money," he said. "The money means nothing to me. What's money at my time of life?" This was the point on which he was most anxious to be believed.

Then their looks said: *What kind of a fool do you take me for?*

He was ruining life for everybody. A housing development next door, hundreds more cars on the roads, snowmobiles, the whine of lawnmowers, barking dogs, the summer-evening air smelling like Burger King was not what Eugene Crockett had in mind in retiring to the country from the city, restoring his antique farmhouse, trimming his woodlots, landscaping his grounds, planting lawns and keeping them like billiard tables. Bob Johnson was saddened by the loss of his old hunting grounds. "What trophies came out of those orchards of yours! Well, that's the way the world is going. It's progress, I suppose. Can't stand in the way of it." Progress: the dirtiest word in his vocabulary! Howard Simms said, "Well, Seth, you won't have to be out on that tractor at all hours of the night anymore." But out on that tractor was where he wanted to be. It was what he was. Or had been.

Ed Smith asked how much it had cost him.

"How much did what cost me?"

"Seth, you and me have lived here all our lives. We both

know how things get done. How much did that zoning variance cost you? Under the table."

What the man meant to express was his cynicism, his inborn suspicion and mistrust of his elected representatives. It never occurred to him that he was implicating his neighbor in bribery and corruption.

Tom Watkins was saying, "Well, Seth, I guess you did the only thing you could. It's not for me to judge you," when his wife Lois burst in with, "Well, I will! You've ruined us all, Seth Bennett. Take a nice rural community and turn it into a country slum."

"Slum?" he said, though he said it softly, not aggressively, not indignantly. "The minimum lots are three acres. And buyers must agree to spend no less than a hundred thousand dollars on their homes." He was not excusing himself. For his part he accepted their fullest reprehension. He just wanted to do what he could to lessen the sorrow they felt for themselves.

"Three acres!" she said with the hauteur of a duchess, and with this scorn too he concurred. Not that her plot was much, if at all, bigger than that, but it was, or had been, bounded on all sides by large holdings, including his, and she had been there long enough to feel a common cause for preservation with those owners of the estates neighboring hers.

"Our life savings are invested in this place," she said, comprehending with a sweep of her hand her two-bedroom bungalow and the one-car garage with its long-outgrown basketball hoop over the door. The humbleness of it accused him as no mansion could have done. He was the spoiler of the American Dream.

"Now?" she said. "Poof! Gone with the wind."

He felt like General Sherman marching through Georgia, or like General Sherman might have felt if confronted by Scarlett on the doorsteps of Tara.

It was while returning home from that encounter that he had his accident. Molly had always said he was going to kill himself on that motorcycle.

He had intended on that afternoon of his accident to make one more stop. This was to have been at the home of people whom he knew well. Thus he knew there had been no death in the family, no divorce, no loss of income. He knew that the "For Sale by Owner" sign in the front yard had been put there by none other than himself. He did not stop, nor even slow down. In fact, he sped up, hoping that he had not been spotted.

He had not been watching the road. He was distracted by an insight into himself. These rounds of his neighbors in which he sought to explain and excuse what he had done and win their forgiveness were not for that purpose at all. Rather the opposite. It was their disapproval he wanted. He would have welcomed being ordered off the property that he had spoiled. He wanted to be blamed so he could blame Janet.

He went off the shoulder of the road at a sharp curve, was thrown from his motorcycle, struck a tree and broke his left arm, the good one.

Now, impatient rather than satisfied with the job he had done, he put down the razor. He loosened the drawstring of his pajamas, dropped his pants and squatted on the toilet seat. Accompanying himself, he sang:

> I'll be with you in apple blossom time.
> I'll be with you to change your name to mine.
> What a wonderful wedding there will be!
> What a wonderful day for you and me!
> Church bells will chime.
> You will be mine.
> In apple blossom time.

He drew from the roll a length of the paper.

With that right hand of his he was clumsy at everything.

I I

"Remember, she's your daughter," said Molly.

"She's yours too. I'm not the only one to blame."

She was helping him dress. Although the wedding party would not begin arriving until late morning, he was putting on his good clothes already rather than go through the struggle twice. With that left arm in a cast bent at a right angle, getting him into a shirt required a contortionist's act for them both. She had to button it for him just as at meals she had to slice his meat as for a child. His helplessness and dependency he blamed on Janet. But for her he would not have gone off the road that day. Ten years of motorcycling with a perfect safety record, despite Molly's prediction that he was going to kill himself on that thing one day.

"But thank you for reminding me," he said. "I'll try not to forget. You might have pointed that out to her while there was still time. I tried."

"Your daughter, I said. Not your slave. She has got a life of her own."

"Yes, and who does she owe it to?"

She went down stiffly on her ruined knees to tie his shoe-laces.

"You can't stand in the path of true love, Seth," she said.

He snorted. "Love! Hah! She'll see how long that lasts."

She was having the trouble she always had getting up off her knees. Looking down, he saw what appeared to be teardrops falling on the toe of his shoe. The readiness of women to weep over anything, or rather over nothing at all, exasperated him.

"Now what's wrong?" he asked as a matter of form.

"Nothing," she said. Which was not what she meant but was what he thought.

"Never mind," she said. Which meant, "You wouldn't understand if I told you."

He was satisfied to think that was probably right.

Molly had asked the foreman of the land-clearing crew to take the day off, spare them the noise, the smoke, the dust.

"I'm sorry, Mr. Bennett," the man said in reporting this to him. "I wish I could oblige. Like the missuz told me, your people have always been married out of the house here, and now this is your last daughter, and all that. But I can't afford to idle these men and these machines. Why, that one bulldozer alone costs a hundred and sixty dollars an hour. And of course I've got no say over the utilities people."

The telephone company was digging trenches for its wires with a rotocutter, the power and light company was digging holes for its poles with an auger. The screech of the one and the roar of the other could be heard from a mile off. Yet though these preparations went on, the building of houses had stalled with two. The promotional literature for the Garden of Eden Estates characterized one as Mediterranean villa, the other as Adirondack lodge. They stood within easy feuding distance of each other. The raw subsoil on which they sat was fertile ground for burdocks and milkweeds while the foundation plantings of azaleas and rhododendrons looked like faded funeral wreaths. Although his prospective son-in-law had brought a stream of prospective buyers to inspect these model homes, no sites had been sold. They would be of course when the market picked up again, but for now there had been a sudden downturn.

"Bad news from Wall Street. High interest rates. Tight mortgage money. You got out just in time, Dad."

"No apologies," he shouted to the foreman. "I appreciate your position. You know how women are. Sentimental. No head for practical affairs. You've got your job to do. You carry right on. The bride and groom will still be able to hear each other say, 'I do.'"

On his way to the cemetery he passed the beehives.

In blossom-time, plying back and forth daylong laden with nectar, the bees had distilled and stored honey enough for themselves and for him to market, meanwhile incidentally pollinating apple blossoms as uncountable as the stars of the Milky Way. Thousands upon thousands of untiring helpers he had. They were his indispensable partners. In exchange for their services to him he kept their hives clean, protected them against the diseases they were prone to, in lean years wintered them over with sugar syrup. More than partners, they were his friends. He could let them crawl on his bare skin without fear of getting stung.

Once, or rather always before, the hives had teemed like tenements, abuzz inside and with gossipy gatherings on the stoops. Now they stood empty, deserted. He had advertised them for sale but had found no buyer, another sign of the disappearance of orchardmen — a vanishing species. Their source of livelihood gone, the bees had left in search of another. They would have to adapt themselves to strange nectars, though it was to be doubted that the clearing of the land hereabouts would leave blossoms of any sort for years to come.

In the center of the cemetery stood a lone apple tree. Though he himself had planted it, it was old now, and time had thinned its blossoms as it had his hair. Its branches overhung several closely spaced graves. He had pruned the tree, sprayed it; he had not picked it. Its fruit had been allowed to fall — an annual offering to those who rested below. Golden Delicious they were, and on the ground they were a shower of gold. He called it "the family tree." With him gone, no one would tend it anymore and its fruit would grow cankered and gnarled, for with him the Bennett line came to its end. It seemed to him more than ever fitting that on his and Molly's tombstone the surname should have been left off, for they were not passing it on. Beneath stones bearing their married names their daughters would lie dispersed among their husbands' family plots.

With no sons that was bound to happen. Though it was painful, he accepted that. It did not mean that the world, his world, had come to an end. He was old enough to have known varieties of apples that were now extinct. The Rock Pippin, the Repka Malenka, the Buckingham — the list was a long one. They had been hybridized with other kinds and in the marriage their names were changed. But their offspring were still apples. With him not just the name but the life that the name had stood for was dying out.

He had not bred true to type, and his failure made him feel beholden to these, his and his daughters' ancestors. He did not regret having had daughters but he could not help regretting having had the daughters he had. He blamed each for the dereliction of all, particularly Janet, the one given the opportunity to redeem the others and make herself — as she had been until then — the apple of his eye. A sense not of the impermanence of life but of his long lineage, of his deep-delving roots in this consecrated earth, was what he had always felt when straying among these graves. Now he would come here no more until he came forever.

"Speak now, or forevermore hold your peace."

The Wedding March had been rendered on the wheezy old parlor organ, pedal-power supplied by the undertaker, while the bride descended the stairs on her father's arm. Now facing the preacher, beside the groom, stood his Best Man, at the bride's side her father, the preacher's father-in-law. Seated on chairs and on the sofa were the wedding party: the bride's mother, her sisters, the parents of the groom, and Pete Jeffers. He had been invited to stay on in the house while looking for a new job. Farther to the north, out of commuting distance, there were still working orchards, and he had made several trips up there. He had found no opening. He was here now as a wedding guest against his will, and it showed in his illness-at-ease.

"But, Seth, it's a family affair," he protested.

"You're family. Or might have been. You had my blessing."

He was determined that Pete be present both as a punishment to him for having been so unenterprising and as the embodiment of his own disappointment. But though he was demanding a favor of Pete, and a painful one at that, he had not ingratiated himself when, after a second tumbler of it, the hundred-proof homemade applejack began to talk: "It's all your fault."

"Seth, you can lead a horse to water —"

"Lead a horse to water! You never even got a halter on her. How many nights did I take Molly out to some boring movie, even a double feature, only to come home and find you in bed fast asleep? Did you ever even get as far as holding hands with her? Ten thousand trees yours for the asking and all you did was drag your feet! Well, many happy returns of the day. I've got to get through it, and you're going to too."

To make himself heard above the din outside the preacher had to raise his voice. A bulldozer was uprooting a tenacious tree with a squeal like an elephant on the rampage.

"Knoweth any person present cause why this man and this woman should not be joined in holy matrimony?

"Speak now, or forevermore hold your peace."

Ranked like the members of a jury, the bygone Bennetts framed on the walls frowned down upon the proceedings. Forced forevermore to hold their peace, they looked to their descendant to speak now for them one and all, for all as one. The living members of the cast seemed breathlessly fearful that he might. The urge to do so was powerful. It was all he could do to restrain himself. He let his moment pass, but he had enjoyed it while it lasted. It pleased him to feel the power he had to scare them, their inability to predict him.

He had been through all this twice before. Now to come was the part he dreaded most. It had been bad enough the two previous times. On this, the third and last, he was not sure but what his tongue would cleave to his palate, unwilling, unable to utter the hateful words. And so, for a time, while all hung upon his silence, it did.

"Who giveth this woman to be married to this man?"

The father of the bride looked around him as though seeking a way out of his strait. He surveyed his kith and kin assembled for this joyous occasion. It brought to mind, like viewing the negative and the positive of a photograph, the family album he had planned for himself. Too numerous to be housed under one roof, his was to have been a compound of kin, a colony with a common aim. No parceling of the property among them. Its bounty would belong to all as one, and in years when the harvest was bad the hardship would be shared equally. The girls would babysit for one another and for advice on child-rearing would come next door to their mother. In time the school bus would again stop to take on in the morning and in the afternoon to discharge their most precious crop. Farm-reared, free-ranging, healthy, happy boys and girls, brothers, sisters and cousins, with no other wish in the world than to follow in their parents' and grandparents' footsteps. Abraham and Sarah he and

Molly would be to their big brood. His last years would be his ripest, his harvest-time. He overseeing all: young minds seeking his advice, young arms carrying out his directives. More fruit than ever the farm would produce. On Sundays the women working happily in the old kitchen preparing the weekly family feast, he in his place at the head of the table, bestowing his benedictions, dispensing his wisdom, the table-talk about the weather, the prospects for the crop, the market for it, the women as interested in the matter as their men. In the lives of his successors, they living theirs as he had lived his, he would live on, a recurrent reincarnation. Garden of Eden indeed!

The work outside came to an abrupt stop. Lunchtime.

"I do," he said in the sudden silence.

"Then I pronounce you . . ."

The grandfather's clock struck: twelve funereal knells. It ought to have stopped forever then, its hands folded together upon this moment that put an end to all its many yesterdays.

Corks popped, glasses were filled and toasts raised to the long life and happiness of the newlyweds. He set his down untouched, and there it stayed, going flat, through the rest of the celebrations. The bride sliced and served the cake.

"Dad," Arnold, the unctuous undertaker, said brightly.

He hated to have his sons-in-law call him "Dad," as all did. It was a familiarity, a presumption. They had married his daughters, not him. To add to his annoyance was the fact that "Dad" was what he had tried to get Pete to call him. It was a way of insinuating him into the family. Tried and failed. Pete refused. He wondered why.

"Maybe it was what he called his father," Molly suggested.

"His father's dead."

"That he's dead doesn't mean he's replaceable," she said.

"Dad, now that you're free —"

He hated to be told that he was now free. "Free" meant idle, useless, finished. He longed for the lost servitude in which his life had been spent, for that was his life, and he feared the emptiness of however much future was his.

"— you ought to travel. Get away from here while all this clatter and mess is going on. You can afford to and you have certainly earned it. Or better still, why not buy yourself a nice little condominium somewhere in the Sun Belt and spend your winters down there? Be good for Mom's poor knees. They've got these retirement set-ups (he hated the word "retirement") with social rooms, entertainment, dining commons, organized group activities, excursions. Never a dull moment."

Shuffleboard. Ping-Pong. Bridge. Bingo. Exercise classes. Arts and crafts. Disneyland. This after life as a man, doing a man's work, feeding people, his own man, independent.

"Dad? Did you hear me?"

"There's nothing wrong with my hearing, thank you." In fact his hearing was impaired from the years of exposure to the piercing noise of the pesticide sprayer. Sometimes it seemed he heard only what he would rather not hear.

"Oh. I just thought that with all the racket outside . . ."

"I heard you."

"Well, just a suggestion. Think it over."

He hated to be told to think something over.

Asked recently by somebody, "Did you hear what happened?" he had snapped, "No, and don't tell me. I hate everything that happens."

If people thought he was churlish that suited him just fine. He had earned it. Or had had it thrust upon him.

The undertaker retreated with the air of someone who had tried to stroke a pet and been snarled at.

"Don't bury me yet. Hear?" he called. "I'm still alive!" It was saying so that made him wonder.

Presently the happy couple approached him, arm in arm.

"Papa, we've got something to tell you," said Janet.

"Call me 'Father,'" he said. "You're not a little girl any-more." What he was saying was, "You're not *my* little girl any-more."

"Very well, Father. Have it your way."

"Hah! When have I had my way?"

To her husband she said, "Do you want to be the one to tell him or shall I?"

He hated this new wifely deference of hers. She seemed to have just been put on a leash, and to like it. To think that she must ask her husband's permission to tell him something!

Her husband gave her his consent with a nod.

"Well," she said, "we thought you would like to know that we have decided to take the name Evans-Bennett."

Like to know! *Like* to know! The thought of his name at-tached like a tail to that detested one! Meant as a sop, it was insult added to injury. He considered for a moment not saying what he felt like saying, then said it:

"I suppose there is nothing I can do to stop you."

Her eyes flashed with hurt and anger.

Meanwhile:

"Well, if you won't I will."

Mr. and Mrs. Minister were quarreling. How unbecoming! How inappropriate to the occasion! What an ill-timed show of marital disharmony to set before the newlyweds!

"Please, Trevor. No. Another time. Not now."

"Why not now? What better time? Who knows when we will all be together like this again? When the hen lays the cock will crow."

Their dispute having been made public, the husband felt obliged to explain it. His side of it, that was.

"Family. Friends of the family," he said. "I have an announcement to make. One which, in her modesty, my dear wife does not want me to make. But I, in my immodesty, must overrule her. For the first time, you understand. My aim is to add joy to this joyful occasion by announcing that we are expecting."

Until now his grandchildren had been fatherless in his imagination. Oh, they would require fathers, as the blossom required the pollen, but they were their mothers' children, fruit of his fruit. They had been faceless. Now in the features of his sons-in-law he saw theirs prefigured. They were to have been a prolongation of his life; this announcement of the first one's coming seemed to signal its approaching end. This child would bear no resemblance to him. He would have no share in the shaping of it. It would be a town child and would speak another language. Onto his stock had been grafted varieties alien to it.

Bitterness flooded him as he surveyed the gulf between his feelings and those he was supposed to be feeling on this occasion. A principal in these proceedings — their very source — he was no part of them. He was the father of the bride, an enviable role — for him a bitter disappointment. He had now married off all his three daughters, one of life's major milestones — to him a mockery. He had just learned that he would soon be a grandfather, another joy — for him joyless. He was now retired from his long years of hard labor, and he was burdened by his leisure. He might almost be called wealthy from the sale of the farm, and the money was hateful to him. This wedding was his wake.

Flashbulbs were gaily popping and this made him leaf back through that family album in his mind. Beneath the married faces of his daughters he saw the blossoms on the bough that they had been. He recalled the many times they had been tucked in bed and allowed to fall asleep before Molly and he went out on the tractor and the sprayer and spent the night in the orchard. They would leave them purring like kittens, yet while they worked they worried every minute that one of them might wake up sick or frightened and wake the others and they not find their parents there to comfort them, and he remembered one night when Molly dozed off at the wheel and woke up inches short of going over the cliff at the edge of the land and they had dashed to the house as if they had indeed orphaned the children.

When the applause and the congratulations had died down, Ellen, in something like anguish, said to Janet, "I tried to stop him. You heard me. It would have kept for another time. This is your day."

It took Janet a moment to understand. When she did she gasped. When she recovered her breath she said indignantly, "How could you think that I would resent it? How could you think that I would be so petty? *That* is what I resent! Oh, how *could* you?"

She was fighting back tears.

"My day," she said bitterly. "My day. Come, Rodney. Let's get out of here."

The time had come for him to spring his surprise.

"May I have your attention, please?" he said. "Will you be seated? Thank you."

He put on his eyeglasses and took from their folder a sheaf of papers. Then, "As my son-in-law, the Reverend, said earlier in making his announcement of an addition to the family, 'Who knows when we will all be together like this again?'"

It would not be anytime soon. A solitude had already settled upon the house. Once Pete was gone, as he would be shortly, Molly and he would be alone. The girls, feeling themselves and their husbands unwelcome and out of place, would seldom visit. Their old home was theirs no longer. It was not his either. He was in it only on tenure. It was not even his to bequeath.

"The last will and testament of Seth Bennett," he read aloud. He paused for effect.

His eyeglasses were for reading. He had worn them for years. Thus this was not the first time that, when he looked up from the page, his sight swam. But with those words of his still echoing, it was the first time that this vagueness of vision made it seem as though the world was receding from him, or he from it. He had meant to stun his audience, and so he had, but the one most stunned was himself. It was his obituary he was reading.

"I, Seth Bennett, residing in the town of New Utrecht, Columbia County, State of New York, do hereby make, publish and declare this my last will and testament, hereby revoking all testamentary instruments heretofore made by me.

"I direct that all my just debts and funeral expenses be paid as soon after my decease as may be practicable. I further direct that all estate, transfer and inheritance taxes, addressed with respect to my estate herein disposed of . . ."

Ordinarily so remote-sounding, pertaining to somebody else, the legalese took on a nearness felt by all, himself most of all.

"I give, devise and bequeath all my property, both real and personal —"

That was the standard form. He would leave no real property.

"— which I may own at the time of my death, wheresoever situate, to my beloved wife, Molly Bennett."

He laid the paper aside and held up the three envelopes.

To all he said, "These contain three checks, one for each of my daughters." To them he said, "Will you please come and take them."

They hesitated. None wanted to be the first to show an eagerness to claim hers, just as, after having done so and resumed their seats, none wanted to be the first to open hers and exhibit a greedy curiosity.

He might have said, "Well. Open them," and with that paternal command have relieved them of responsibility. But he was enjoying their discomfort. He was teasing them, tormenting them. He was corrupting them, and the one whose heart their corruption was breaking was himself.

"All together they represent the entire proceeds from the sale of the farm," he said. "I want no part of it. You will find that they are all equal when you compare them."

"Oh, Father!" the elder two exclaimed in tones of injured innocence, shock. Janet said nothing, but resentment was all over her face.

It was Doris who yielded first to the urge to look. The amount of the check made her gasp. She showed it to her husband for him to see their newfound wealth. Freed from restraint by her sister's example, Ellen opened hers.

"Oh! Father!" said both.

"You'd have gotten it sooner or later. Better sooner. I don't want to have to feel that you're just waiting for me to die." Having settled their inheritance upon them, he could die whenever it suited him as far as they were concerned, or live as long as he might.

They hung their heads in sorrow and in shame for him at having such unnatural feelings imputed to them.

Janet's envelope remained unopened. She now rose, tore it in half and let the pieces fall to the floor.

Her final act before leaving home was to kiss him goodbye. It was a kiss on the cheek but it pierced his heart, as it was meant to do, an icy kiss, not a token of love but the discharge of her last duty as his daughter.

The land-clearing crew had quit work for the day. Inside and outside all was quiet. The ever-burning fires of the trees smoldered on and even in the house the air smelled of their smoke. The sun had set and the light was beginning to wane. He sat alone in the dusky parlor amid the leavings of the party, dirty plates, empty glasses. Molly was off somewhere, no doubt shedding her mother's tears of joy over the marriage of her baby daughter and of sorrow over her leaving home. He toyed with the figurine from the wedding cake of the bride and groom. In her haste to get away from the home he had made hateful to her, Janet had left it behind.

Pete appeared, carrying the suitcase and the duffelbag with which he had arrived a year earlier.

"So soon?" he said.

"The sooner the better. I've got my fortune to make. And that's going to take some doing."

"Setting off so late in the day? Don't you want to wait until morning at least?"

"I can still make two hundred miles before bedtime."

"Where will you go?"

"I'm thinking of Washington. That's still a big apple-producing state. There ought to be a place for me out there. I'll write when I'm settled."

"I know how painful it must be to pull up your roots and transplant yourself. But you're young. You can send down new roots. I'll give you the highest recommendation. How are you fixed for money?"

"Got a pocketful. You've paid me well, and you know I'm not a big spender. But thanks for asking. You've been good to me, Seth. Like a father."

"I hope you make that fortune. I wish you a long and happy life."

"I've said goodbye to Molly."

"We'll miss you."

"And I will never forget you. No, don't follow me out to the car. We'll say goodbye here."

"Goodbye, son. Bless you."

Alone again in the failing light he considered the prospect before him. At its end, both near and far, stood that tombstone with his name on it and its uncompleted dates. His remaining years had become too many to endure, too few to cling to.

Outside, the eddying smoke dimming the air gave to things an aspect of unreality. He settled himself on the ground and leaned his back against his tombstone. He raised the pistol to his head, closed his eyes, fired — and missed his aim.

That right hand of his was good for nothing.

# A Weekend
# in the Country

I HAVE BEEN in some of the finest homes in New England, upstate New York. In them? I have been all through them, top to bottom, basement to attic. While others play golf or go fishing on their weekends I go house-hunting.

For the class of estates I get shown you do not just walk into the agent's office from off the street. Meg — my wife — says, "Pinnacle Realty? I have a call for you from Mr. Joseph Preston. He will be right with you. Mr. Preston, sir, your party is on the line. The green button."

She hands me the phone.

I say, "Next weekend? No, afraid not. I must be in Bermuda for a conference then. The following weekend? Let me just check my calendar. Yes. That will be fine. Miss St. Johnsbury, will you set up the appointment, please?"

"What sort of property are you interested in, Mr. Preston?"

"Quiet."

"Period or modern?"

"As long as it's quiet."

My favorite seasons for house-hunting are when the apple trees are in blossom and when the leaves change color. Whoever has not seen New England in the fall has missed one of life's beauties. And when the orchards flower in the Hudson Valley it is Christmas in May.

On our weekends we put up at cozy country inns. We choose them by consulting our well-worn copy of Wilfred Milford's *Cozy Country Inns.* The ones we choose are those not listed by Wilfred.

I sign the register.

The innkeeper says, "Oh, Mr. Milford! It's an honor to have you with us!" Then rather ruefully, "We are not in your book, you know."

I say, "I am doing research for a new edition. There will be changes. There will be some new names. And some of the old ones will be dropped."

You are given the best room in the house. The chef knocks himself out for you. You want yours medium rare? You get it medium rare. You can just picture the fellow out in the kitchen hovering over that hot grill like a bird on the nest.

We sometimes used to return to the same inn for a second stay while being shown around by a different realtor in the area. The way the restaurant critics in the *New York Times* do. You're sampling further before deciding how many stars to award. Then you really get the red carpet treatment.

We don't do that anymore. Not after the time the innkeeper said that since our first visit a fellow impersonating me had been there. He was given the bum's rush. That might have happened the other way round. Nowadays we don't push our luck.

It is important in house-hunting to make the right impression. It is a matter of both your air and your appearance. I drive a Toyota, carry a Bic pen, wear a Timex. Obviously I could drive a Maserati, sport a Mont Blanc, lift my gold cufflink to reveal a Patek Philippe, only I've got more refined taste as well as better sense. Who wants to get ripped off, be kidnapped and held for several millions in ransom? As for my air: would I be wasting my weekend looking at seven-figure offerings unless I could afford one?

Not only do you tour beautiful homes, there is no better way to see the countryside than with a real estate agent. They know every road and in chauffeuring you from one place to the next they choose the most attractive. You are spared the sight of car graveyards, landfills, trailer camps. Unfortunately, even the choicest areas do have such eyesores. You show your appreciation by remarking how unspoiled it is hereabouts. You are assured that with the recently adopted zoning regulations it will remain so.

Just as appealing as fine architecture and beautiful landscape in house-hunting is the human interest. It is a sad fact, but true that most houses come on the market through the breakup of the family, and of course no families break up more than those of the rich and the famous. You meet the most interesting people, the most newsworthy. You don't have to buy the scandal sheet at the checkout counter; you can shake the hand of the best-selling author caught with his pants down, his fifth marriage on the skids, forced to sell to pay that alimony. When the owners are people you never heard of because they have lived since the *Mayflower* dropped anchor in well-heeled privacy the agent opens their skeleton cupboard for you to peek into. He or she wants you to know that the reason for selling is not that something is wrong with the house but rather that something is wrong with the family. You get the lowdown. Insanity. Hushed-up embezzlement. Bankruptcy. The extinction of an old clan, the surviving representatives seated in the drawing room like the last pair of passenger pigeons while you inspect the manor.

On your drive to the next offering after the palace whose owner recently received a life sentence the agent says, "Poor dear Mrs. Delaney! All alone in that big house, except for the servants. It is several years since one of her doctors asked how she was and she said she was happy now to have settled all her children in nursing homes. Say nothing to her about buying the place. It's been in the family since the Creation. They trace their line to Adam and Eve. It's the great-grandchildren who have put it on the market. Pretend that she knows you. She won't know that she doesn't. She'll invite us to tea. Just don't bring up the subject of the Boer War. She's quite bitter about that."

On your typical weekend in the country you are shown maybe six houses. You don't just breeze through twenty rooms, guest cottage, stables, kennels, pool, four-car garage, the caretaker's apartment over it. You're in no hurry. You're enjoying your private guided tour. Seeing how the other half lives. Except in your bracket the fraction is a great deal smaller than half. You show your seriousness by turning on faucets to test the pressure. You ask about local taxes. Heating costs. Train service. The availability of domestic help. To the agent you're the perfect prospect. You like everything you're shown, and you're not easily pleased. But the retirement home you're looking for will be your first, and you want to make sure it's your last.

At the end of your weekend in the country the agent says, "If you're interested in any of the properties you've been shown, all have been inspected, appraised, approved, and we will be glad to help negotiate the mortgage with our local bank at quite attractive rates."

I say, "I have never in my life bought anything on credit. You won't find me in Dun and Bradstreet."

There is no bill to pay when we check out of the inn.

We get away in time to beat the traffic down to the city.

Monday morning bright and early it's back to sorting mail.

# September Song

WHO HAS NEVER DAYDREAMED that the phone will ring and the caller be an old lover?

Virginia Tyler was now seventy-six, and that fantasy, foolish to start with, had become embarrassing. Yet though it was twenty years since she had heard from John Warner, sometimes, sitting by the fire at night and studying the flames, it returned to her. She would have to shake her silly old head to clear it of its nonsense.

And then it happened! As she would say in her letter to the children announcing her intention to divorce their father and remarry, her heart leapt. She had thought it had withered and died, and been half glad it had — unruly thing! She did not know until then that it had lain dormant, like those seeds from the tombs of the pharaohs that, when planted, blossom and bear.

Toby was in the next room, doing his daily crossword puzzle.

"Is it for me?" he called.

Outwardly calm, she said, "No, it's for me." Inwardly, both ecstatic and furious, she said, "It's for *me! Me!*" His smug assumption that every call was for him!

Into the receiver she said, "Hold on. I'll check it out upstairs."

The phone had to be left off the hook so as not to break the connection. But she had no fear that Toby might listen in on the conversation. He was incurious about her private affairs. As far as he was concerned, she had no private affairs, no life of her own apart from his. And he was right: she didn't have, though she had once had, and a wild one it was.

It is said that as we die our lives pass in review before our eyes. It was as she was brought back to life that Virginia Tyler's did.

Listening to that voice on the phone, she was lifted into the clouds. She saw herself in flight, alone, at the controls of her plane.

To join her lover she had taken flying lessons. Her friends all thought she had gone out of her mind. At her age! Then already a grandmother!

"This grandmother has sprouted wings! I'm as free as a bird!" she said as she touched down on her solo flight.

Toby, who had a fear of flying, was proud of her. He gave a party in her honor to celebrate the event. Actually, though she pooh-poohed it in others, she too was afraid of flying. Her fear was a part of her excitement, and a source of pride. For her love's sake she risked life and limb. Winging her way to him, earth-free, added zest to the affair, and youth and glamour to her image of herself. Outward bound, leaving home, she was a homing pigeon. Her path was so direct the plane might have been set on automatic pilot, guided by the needle of her heart.

John too was a licensed pilot. It was he who first interested her in flying. They were winged; they were mating birds. They nested in many far-away places. She did not share Toby's interest in cathedrals, art museums, yet though she resented his pleasure in traveling by himself, his lone European pilgrimages gave her the opportunity to be with John. He would tell his wife that he was off to a conference in Cleveland, Birmingham, Trenton. She would wonder why they always chose such dreary places, and decide to stay at home. The lovers would alight for a week on Nantucket, in New York City. Registering at a hotel as husband and wife, answering to the name "Mrs. Warner," never lost its thrill for her.

Planes were for rent at the local airport. Her visits to Boston to see her mother became more frequent. Toby was pleased that she and her mother now got along so much better than always before. She said that now that her mother was old she felt she must make up to her for the bad feeling between them over the years. Her mother said, "I'm just your excuse to fly that fool airplane. At your age!"

On her forty-eighth birthday Toby gave her a Piper Cub. That brought her a twinge of remorse.

"Now that you own your own plane you're flying not more but less — hardly at all," he said. "Don't you like it? Did I buy the wrong kind?"

"Oh, I'll get back to it in time," she said.

She wondered at his lack of suspicion, and his misplaced trust in her shamed her. It also rather irritated her. Was it that she was too old, too long settled, too domesticated to be suspected of any wrongdoing? She was so conscious of her guilty happiness she felt it must show in telltale ways of which she herself was unaware. She had read *Madame Bovary* and remembered Emma's saying to herself in awe, "I am an adulteress!" She felt transfigured, hardly knew herself. This alteration in her *must* show, if not to Toby then to others. She half-hoped it did! Her dread of disclosure had to contend with a wild wish to have the whole world know. They took her for a middle-aged matron, conventional, unadventurous, yoked to a dull, inattentive husband. They should only know! As for Toby, he took her for granted. Wouldn't it give him a shaking up if she were to tell him!

They never considered getting divorced and marrying each other. As she could see, his deception troubled John, but the guilt he felt was as much toward his son for what he was doing to his mother as toward her. Bruce adored his mother. At twenty-three he showed no inclination toward any other woman. It was doubtful that he would ever marry. He adored his father, too. Adored him as the consort of his queen. Marcia was a fiercely proud woman — perhaps even proud of enduring a marriage that went against her grain. To be divorced would humiliate her.

She too balked at the step. Toby was a one-woman man and without her would be helpless in a hundred little ways. She pitied him — another reason for not loving him — but while it often grated her, she took a certain satisfaction in his dependence upon her. She was fond of Toby, in her way. Some of his habits irritated her: his reading at meals, his smoking in the car, etc., but she was fond of him — or so she kept telling herself. She did not love him, but she shrank from hurting him — or from the guilt she would feel if she did. She told herself that given the choice between her deceiving him and her leaving him, he would choose to have her stay. She had her children, too, whom she hesitated to shock, whose censure she dreaded. And she feared her mother, a Boston puritan, one of a long line, with strict views on sex, marriage, duty, self-denial. A formidable woman. Once when somebody said to her offhandedly, "Well, nobody's perfect," she took it as a personal affront. Drawing herself up stiffly, she said, without a trace of self-irony, "*I* am. If I weren't I'd change."

And both were daunted by the prospect of such upheaval, the loss of disapproving friends, the sheer undertaking of creating a new life in a new place. Bad though they might be, old habits were hard to break, and fresh frontiers, while beckoning, were also scary when you reached a certain age. It made you feel old, cowardly and lazy to admit it, but it was easier to rock along with things as they were.

Still, despite all these deterrents, she would have made the break if he had urged it. But, as when they danced, he led, she followed.

"If only both of *them* would find others," he said, which would not only have freed them but salved their consciences. "But Marcia doesn't like men. Except Bruce."

"And Toby has got me," she said. "Old Faithful. Or so he thinks."

To receive letters from each other in secret both rented boxes in post offices where they were unknown. Yet it all ended when Marcia found one of her letters to him. She was almost ready to excuse his carelessness. He had been unable to destroy it! Any one of her letters to him was a giveaway. They were not the gushings of a girl with a crush on, say, a professor. They were her pillow talk, the uninhibited outpourings of a long-somnolent woman to the Prince Charming who had awakened her with his kiss. Asbestos sheets rather than writing paper would have better suited their contents.

In his last letter he wrote that he had promised Marcia never to see her again. But his love was undying.

The Piper Cub was sold.

Her wings had been clipped.

Over the succeeding years:

The children all left home.

Married.

Had children.

Toby retired.

He grew increasingly hard of hearing and that made him less talkative than ever. One mate's deafness made the other one dumb. She pitied him for his infirmity, yet his refusal to get a hearing aid exasperated her. She had to repeat everything she said to him. It was so frustrating! She knew that his resistance to a hearing aid was not because he was vain of his appearance. Of that he was all too careless. It was that to wear one would be a constant reminder, like eyeglasses, false teeth, of decay. She was ashamed of her irritation with him, but that did not keep her from feeling it.

She knew that people long together grew impatient with one another's ways and weaknesses and magnified them out of all proportion. His chronic sinusitis was an affliction he had not sought, yet his honking into his handkerchief so annoyed her that sometimes she had to leave the room. It was he who should leave the room.

He had always been bookish; his hardness of hearing made him burrow still deeper into books, leaving her more than ever to herself. One winter evening, snow flying, wind moaning, the two of them sat in silence before the fire, he reading, unconscious of, indifferent to whatever she might or might not be doing. To see just how long this could go on she sat there for hours. At last she rose, took his book from him and tossed it into the fire.

"Now what did you do that for?" he wondered aloud as she made her way upstairs.

Now had come the call she had waited twenty years for, never expecting it. It was as though some dear one had come back from the dead. And as though she had too.

"That was John Warner on the phone," she said. The care with which she enunciated the name conveyed the need she had felt to place the person.

"John Warner?"

"Mmh. Remember him?"

"John Warner ... Oh, yes. Yes. Long time no see. What's with him?"

"His wife has died."

That would make it sound as though his wife had *just* died. That he was newly in need of sympathy, condolence. But she had died three years ago. Three years! Oh, why had he waited so long to call her? Three precious years! All that time lost when there was so little time to lose, to live! Yet she could explain his hesitancy to herself. She could imagine him longing to call her but thinking, "After all these years? She has forgotten you, you sentimental old fool. No doubt she replaced you with another lover. You're too old for this nonsense — and so is she. What right have you to disturb her settled life? There is not an ember left of what was once a fire — not on her side. With three children she's a grandmother many times over — a great-grandmother by now."

But he had called! He had overcome his fear of looking ridiculous, of being laughed at, rejected. He had trusted in her faithfulness, had trusted that she would respond. He alone of all the world believed she still had a heart that did not just pump but palpitated.

"Oh, dear! Poor man. Yes. His wife was a very beautiful woman."

"Mmh. You have no trouble remembering her, I see."

She was doubly jealous.

"He says he would like to meet me. In the old days he used to be rather ... fond of me." This last she said in a musing tone, as though after all these years just now recalling it. "If you can believe that." Her little jab was lost on him.

"Where is he?"

"In Boston."

"Then of course you must go. Poor man! To lose his wife."

A meeting between an elderly widower, recently bereaved, still in mourning, and a onetime friend who just happened to be of the opposite sex, a seventy-six-year-old great-grandmother, contentedly married for half a century: what could be more innocent?

She resented the assumption that her capacity for love, for adventure — even for mischief — had been worn away by the abrasion of time. It had just been rekindled. What the world would ridicule as her silliness aroused her defiance. No fool like an old fool, all would say; act your age. That was just what she was doing. Who better than she knew her age? The stopwatch was running, and her countdown to zero was for a launch.

"But you're a woman of seventy-six!" Those were his first words to her when, on her return home from Boston, she asked him for a divorce so that she might marry John Warner. The trip had been like a weekend pass from prison. Now she was demanding her parole. She felt she owed no apology. She had earned her freedom by her years of good behavior.

John showed his age and she was glad he did. She had feared that he would find her too old. He did not try to tell her that she had not changed, and she was glad of that too. He accepted her as she was. He said, "You look wonderful!" And his eyes shone with a light that she had not seen in a man's since last looking into his.

They drove down to the Cape, to his saltbox on the shore. They strolled on the beach. Arm in arm. Together they prepared the meal and dined at home. He was still all that he had been, and he made her feel that she was too. A few wrinkles — what were they? The intervening years vanished as though at the wave of his wand. It was she — *she!* — across the table from him, in the candlelight's flattering glow. No book lay on the surface separating them. She did not mind his self-assurance; she liked his certainty that she was his.

He had let her know over the phone something of what she might expect if she agreed to meet him. He held her hand, and it was the splicing of a long-severed electric connection, the current restored; but he did not want just to hold hands. He paid her court, turning upon her all his charm, his wit, but briefly — telegraphing his intentions. She appreciated his gallantry, but she must not prolong it. There was not time for coyness. He had a lot to accomplish in a short while — more, indeed, than she guessed. For just picking up where they had broken off all those years ago and carrying on as before was not what he had in mind. He had in mind much more than that.

After dinner they danced. He had mapped out his flattering but needless campaign of conquest down to orchestrating on tape the background music. They swayed to:

> You were meant for me.
> I was meant for you.

To:

> Although you belong to somebody else,
> Tonight you belong to me.

To — in the sultry voice of Marlene Dietrich:

> Falling in love again —
> Oh, what am I to do?

Long as I'm near you
I can't help it.

Being the music of their youth, it made them feel young. Until the finale, in the cracked old voice of Walter Huston — his proposal to her in song:

For it's a long long time from May to December
But the days grow short when you reach September

She needed no persuading to spend those remaining days with him.

"But you're a great-grandmother!" said Toby.

"I do not need to be told my age. Nor that I am not acting it. I see it in the mirror. I feel it in my joints. I am an old woman. But I am still a woman. A woman in love. I am not afraid of making a fool of myself. What you are afraid of is my making you look foolish. You won't miss me. You will still have your books, your slippers and your pipe.

"Your first words to me ought to have been, 'I love you. Don't leave me. Give me a chance to prove my love to you and to win back yours.' It would have done you no good. It's too late in the day for that. But it is what you ought to have said."

"Well! This has certainly been a whirlwind romance."

"I liked him when I knew him before. Now, as you have so chivalrously pointed out, I have got no time to lose."

In truth, she both did and did not feel her age. Her years with Toby after the loss of John had dragged by, they had piled up. And yet in their very sameness they ran together, uncountable, all one. They were easily shed. They were like a sleep. A sleep from which she had now awakened.

"So," she said. Discussion was at an end, it was time now for decision. "Are you going to give me what I want, or do you mean to contest it?"

"Well . . . If that is what you want . . ."

So that was how much she meant to him! Not worth putting up the least fight for. Her heart sped on wings to her old, her new lover.

Then her conscience told her that she was being unfair. If he was so readily acquiescent it was because he had been stunned, crushed. In just one minute, the duration of an earthquake, his familiar world had crumbled.

"This is a pretty big step," he said. "Are you sure of your own mind? Don't you want to think it over?" Then with a feeble attempt at humor, "Lots of auld lang syne riding on this, old friend."

She was moved, but moved to pity, not to a change of heart. That was no longer hers to change.

She wrote the children, braving their condemnation for her faithlessness to their father, their embarrassment over her geriatric folly. That she not seem still more ridiculous than she did, she had to reveal to them her affair of long ago with the same man. This was not someone new to her. To confess herself a one-time adulteress to her children was preferable to having them think she was so depraved as to fall illicitly in love for the first time at her age. All three approved, her daughter applauded, even reveled in the revelation of her former affair. Poor Toby! What treacherous little beasts children were! It made her wonder about the example she was setting her daughter. She had had misgivings about that marriage, and about what its breakup would mean to her grandchildren. Their encouragement brought with it a pang. It showed how pitifully apparent to them over the years had been her need for warmth, her lack of love. It was an acknowledgment of how little time she had left in which to find a crumb of the true staff of life.

She announced her intention to her brother Thornton. As she had expected, he was scandalized. If she persisted he might well disown her. Thornton had never married; that was how awesome a step he considered holy matrimony to be. He inveighed against divorce. Those of his friends who got one were scratched from his address book. He needed only sandals and a robe to seem like Moses down from the mountaintop bearing the tablets of the law, a list of Thou Shalt Nots inscribed in stone by the fiery forefinger of God. She was not fond of Thornton — he had been a prig from his youth; but she was afraid of him. On matters of devotion and duty he spoke with the voices of both their dead parents, all their ancestors. Yet even the scorching she got from him did not deter her. Thornton was like a firefighter setting a fire around a fire to contain it and let it burn itself out. But her heart's fire blazed on unchecked. Opposition only fanned its flames.

Thornton's opposite was the lady lawyer recommended to her, a specialist in divorce. Separating people was not only her profession, it was her passion.

"Go for it!" she urged. "Never too late to make the break. I know men. Totally inconsiderate. I say being born male is a birth defect."

"It is my intention," she said, "to remarry immediately."

She was not only a fool, said the other woman's look; she was an old fool, of which there was none like.

Toby might have made things extremely unpleasant for her if he had been so inclined. The law, had he invoked it, was on his side. He was the injured party. He might have charged her with desertion, adultery, and have turned her out without a dime. Might have advertised in the town paper, "My wife having left my bed and board, I will no longer be responsible for debts incurred, etc."

He never threatened her with such actions. Instead there would be an equal division of their common property. The house and its furnishings would either be sold or else he would buy it from the estate at the assessed value. She would be financially independent.

"You must be provided for in case this marriage of yours should break up. I owe that to the mother of my children," he said. It was as if he were *her* father, doing his duty by her but washing his hands of an errant child by settling a competence upon her.

"It won't break up," she said.

"One never knows. Ours did. After fifty years."

"Forty-nine," she corrected him. "It only seems longer."

He made one condition, to which she agreed: that she will everything of hers that had once been his in part to their children.

He was being fair. What was unfair was his fairness. His irreproachable uprightness was inhuman. It disarmed her. If he had threatened her, railed at her, she could have defended herself.

Nothing so tried the patience as a saint.

"I'll go by way of —" And he mapped his route. Since growing old they always did this whenever either of them set off alone for someplace. Thus if he or she was not back when expected the state police could be told where to look. He was off now to see his lawyer to draw up the settlement.

She watched him struggle into his coat. Painful arthritis in his left elbow made this difficult for him. But he would refuse her help now. She had forfeited her right to help him. Neither did she straighten his hat, as she had done all their married life. He always got it on slightly crooked. It made him look as if he were headed one way while the rest of him was going off at a tangent. Oh, dear, what would become of him without her to look after him?

She watched him make his way to the garage. He was the picture of rejection. He looked like one of those homeless old men who, bent beneath the weight of their overcoats summer and winter, tramped the highways aimlessly, endlessly. He not only looked like one: his pride, or rather his humiliation — his tattered pride — would never permit him to ask one of the children for a home in his solitary old age.

What would become of him? He could not look after himself. He had never been able to. A more helpless, more dependent man could not be found. Perhaps he would sell the house and go into one of those senior citizens' retirement complexes where the elderlies' wants were all attended to. That thought gave her a wrench. It also held up to her, as in a mirror, an image of herself. In the hunch of his shoulders, in the hang of his head, in his slow gait she saw her own age reflected. Two-thirds of their years they had spent together. She could be sure that in all that time he had never had a thought unfaithful to her. She wished she could think he had. Then she wished she could unwish the wish. It was unworthy of her.

If only John had called her those three years ago! Then the burden of her guilt toward Toby would have been worth it. The saddest of all expressions: if only . . .

He hesitated, stopped, turned around and looked up at the house. "Poor man! To lose his wife," she then recalled his saying of John. For the sake of her belated and sure to be short-lived happiness she was making of him the same lonely object that he had generously pitied in the other man, her lover. Was he hoping that at the last minute she would call him back? Was he thinking of returning, asking her to reconsider? If he did, what would her answer be? A moment ago she would have known, now she was unsure. Oh, let him turn again, get on with it, she prayed. Let him decide for me. But when he did just that she was frightened — frightened of herself.

She felt her purpose falter as the weight of her years settled upon her. It forced from her a sigh of resignation. It sounded to her like her last breath.

From the door she called him back.

Now what? his carriage seemed to say as he plodded up the walk.

"Please, Toby, forgive me, if you can," she said. "I'm sorry. It won't happen again. I'll stay. If you want me."

He nodded wearily.

Well, she asked herself, what warmer welcome back was she entitled to?

Her brother would say, "I'm glad you came to your senses." Her daughter would be disappointed in her, would think she was a fool to throw away her last chance for a little happiness. Her sons would think she had nobly sacrificed herself. There was nothing noble in it. Her heart longed for what it was too old for.

"I'll try harder," he said.

Then it was her turn to nod wearily.

Around her neck she felt a collar tighten. He and she were teamed together to the end by the yoke of years.

But whereas before she had told herself that she might still have quite a long time left to live, she told herself now that at least it would not be for long.

# Mortal Enemies

HE MIGHT BE OLD, his eyesight not quite what it once was, his hand shaky, but he could still shoot. He had killed that woodchuck with a standing shot at a distance of a hundred yards. The one animal he would kill with no intention of eating it. Varmints!

You knew you were alive for another spring with the arrival in the mail of the seed catalogs. You sent off your order: old reliables, newly developed strains. The snow melted, the ground thawed, the grass greened, the trees budded. You emerged from hibernation. So did the woodchucks.

He could picture them waking to their inner alarm clocks, lean and hungry, rubbing the sleep from their eyes, yawning and stretching, issuing forth and finding Burpee's catalog on the stoop. Their mouths would water as they leafed through its full-color pages. Paws lifted, they would pray in chorus that Farmer Thompson had come through the winter and was planting their garden.

You turned your plot and raked it smooth, lined the rows as straight as music paper, planted, fertilized, mulched, watered, weeded. You sweated, you ached. The peas reached out their tendrils and climbed the stakes, blossomed, the pods appeared, swelled. You could hardly wait for them to ripen. Came the day when you decided that tomorrow you would pick your first. You could taste them already. Overnight a woodchuck tunneled under the fence and got them. Those it did not eat it wantonly destroyed. You had been through it times out of number and still you were outraged afresh. Varmints!

For the past few years he had had to give up gardening. Using the turning fork hurt his bad hip. Getting up off his knees had become painful. His name remained on the mailing lists for seed catalogs but the garden plot had gone to weeds. Yet as surely as the woodchucks came aboveground so his old hatred of them resurfaced. He would have exterminated them if he could. Varmints!

This one had moved in some days earlier, settling at the edge of the lawn, and in its self-satisfied survey of things in the morning seemed to think the place belonged to it. It was this that he resented, this impudence.

He had lain in wait for it. They rose early to do their mischief while the world slept. The head appeared like that of a turtle from its shell. Slowly the body emerged. This was an old one, big. Many a garden it must have feasted on. It stood upright on the mound of earth thrown up in digging its hole, looking about. It pleased him to allow it a last moment of smugness. Slowly — for they were alert to the least movement over a long range — he raised the rifle to his shoulder. He aimed, drew a deep breath, released half of it, and squeezed the trigger, timing the shot to go off when the gun barrel wavered back on target. The animal was shaped like a bowling pin and when the bullet struck it toppled over like one.

He leaned the rifle against the wall. Once more it had served him well. He labored across the lawn, a hitch in his gait from favoring that hip.

"Varmint!" he said as he stood over the dead animal. But this time the satisfaction he had always felt before in having eliminated another of the pests did not come to him. He regretted what he had done. He wanted everything to go on living. What they had in common had made peace between him and his old enemy.

# The Dead Languages

FOR A YEAR, since his retirement, he had lived the life of a hermit, his days as alike as if spent in silent prayer, going nowhere, seeing nobody, he who had always loved company, conversation, loved to travel, to exercise his French and his Italian. He was at his desk by eight in the morning, and often he worked past the evening news hour. He, the old newspaperman — byline, Bancroft award — curious about everything, hardly knew what was going on in the world anymore, absorbed as he was in his book. The daylong clackety-clack of the typewriter (he was too old for a word processor) was like that of wheels on rails. He was the engineer, howling through the crossings, drawing behind him his finished chapters like coaches, and now pulling the whistle to announce his arrival at the end of the line. It was from his wife that he learned of the sensational multiple murder that had happened not long ago, right in his own back yard. This was not the first time she had spoken to him about it, she said impatiently. But he never listened to anything she said. She'd might as well be talking to a fencepost.

It was a case to make him lay aside his book (it was all but finished anyway), come out of retirement, and rejoin the world of the living — and the dead. A seventeen-year-old model boy, honor student in the local high school, was charged with slaughtering his family of four: his father, his stepmother, his older brother and his three-year-old half-brother. With his father's 9mm Walther he had pumped fourteen shots into them. As the last person known to have seen the victims alive, he was routinely questioned. He had broken down and confessed to the crime before the night of it was over. He was said to have been motivated by the ambition to inherit the family estate, valued at some hundred thousand dollars, and with it establish a worldwide enforcement agency for the protection of wildlife. The father and the dead brother had been avid hunters.

Ordinarily the argument would have gone like this:

Defense attorney: He did it because he's crazy.

Prosecutor: How do you know he's crazy?

Defense attorney: Because he did it.

Now, on the eve of the trial, the boy's lawyer told reporters that he was not going to enter a plea of insanity. He claimed there was no evidence to convict. What about that confession? Forced.

Interest in the case was widespread. He knew without asking his former editor that, being on the scene, he would be wanted to come out of retirement and cover it. He still kept his old press card, and the name of his paper was enough to gain him a seat in the front row of the press corps.

He had been in the county courthouse many times over the years, for this had been his legal residence while it was still only his summer home, but never before above the ground floor. He had gone there to renew his driver's license, search his deed, apply for a passport, but having been excused from jury duty on the grounds that he alone could do the work he did, he was seeing the courtroom now for the first time. The sight was not reassuring. It was vaulty, full of echoes, and the only air conditioning was a pair of noisy big standing electric fans. The attorneys' backs would be toward you as they questioned the witnesses. Taking notes was going to be a strain.

Even the most lurid of trials had its dull sessions. At times on those somnolent summer afternoons with the fans droning hypnotically, jurors and even members of the press corps nodded. He was too old a hand for that, but he was also old enough not to concoct interest out of nothing and file a daily dispatch to his paper. That hard-earned byline of his was not to be wasted. Often when court was adjourned in the afternoon, he walked past the cub reporters queued up for the courthouse's one telephone, grateful for his age and the status it had gained him, his freedom to judge for himself what was newsworthy.

It was his editor on the phone:

"Where the hell were you yesterday?"

"What was that?"

"WHERE THE HELL WERE YOU YESTERDAY?"

"In court."

"You'd might as well not have been. Didn't you hear the testimony? The kid's lawyer, the one they woke at three in the morning to represent him, was not allowed by the state police sergeant to accompany him into the polygraph room. He was denied his rights. He has gunned down his entire family and he's going to go free. He will even inherit that hundred thousand dollars he was after. Every paper in the state has headlined it. All but ours."

"I've been telling you for years that your hearing was going bad," said his wife. "'I hear what I want to hear,' that's your comeback. Now maybe you'll do something about it."

In the doctor's office he was placed in a soundproof booth wearing earphones. He could see the audiologist through the window.

"Raise your hand if you hear this sound," she said.

Pleased with his performance, he raised his hand as eagerly as a bright schoolchild, until he began to miss the cues.

"Say the word 'grass.' Say the word 'soon.' Say the word 'park.' Say the word 'dark.'"

This went on for half an hour.

"You have lost about fifty percent of your hearing," the doctor told him. "A bit more than that in your right ear, a bit less in the left."

"What can be done for me?"

"Unfortunately, yours is a case in which surgery is not indicated. There is no impairment to the mechanism of the ears. Yours is the commonest kind of hearing loss. Degeneration of the nerves. It says here that you are retired. Did you spend your working life in a noisy environment? A shipyard? An assembly line?"

"At a typewriter."

"That could do it. A low repetitive noise, prolonged over years, can be as destructive as loud ones."

"Is it going to get worse?"

"Most likely. It is sounds in the upper register that you cannot hear. That and certain consonants."

"Good thing then I'm not Polish," he said. He didn't think it was so funny either.

"How could it have happened so suddenly?" he asked.

"It didn't. It has been coming on for a long time. You just didn't become aware of it until it reached a certain point."

He told about the day of discovery when he missed the crucial testimony at the murder trial. Surely that indicated something acute, not chronic, something treatable?

"Think back," said the doctor. "Can you not see yourself cupping your ears, puzzling over what you'd heard, not quite catching the words, asking people what they'd said?"

A mirror had been held up to him.

"Sometimes my hearing is better than at other times," he volunteered hopefully.

The doctor said nothing for what soon came to seem a long time, meanwhile regarding him steadily. At length he asked gravely, "Are you sure of that?"

Initially he was irritated. Who better than he knew the ups and downs of his hearing? But having said with some indignation, "Of course I'm sure," he regretted it when the doctor said, "Quite sure?"

It seemed to him that, just as when he was in the test booth, the doctor was moderating his volume. He thought of the accused boy in the polygraph room attached to monitors as he had just been, and he wished that he was represented by counsel.

"Hmm," the doctor said, and, enunciating all too carefully, "now don't take offense, but I must tell you that intermittent loss and gain of hearing is commonly associated with syphilis."

Going home on the evening train he was not only deaf, he was afflicted with tertiary paresis and had visions of winding up like Maupassant, naked on all fours in a padded cell and finger-painting with his excrement. How long had he had it? How had he gotten it? Had he infected his wife? His children?

"Stan!" (His family doctor, whom he had called at home, out of office hours.) "I've got syphilis!"

"Who says so?"

"The ear doctor. He told me."

"I've been testing you for syphilis for years. Not that I suspected you of having it. Just standard practice."

"Ah, but there are two different tests. He told me. One doesn't show the kind that affects the hearing."

"You're telling me. That's the test you've had. You haven't got syphilis. Meanwhile you seem to be hearing me all right."

"On the phone. With the earpiece pressed close. Then I still do fairly well."

"You haven't got syphilis. You'd have had to have it for years for it to affect your hearing."

"The doctor says I've been losing my hearing for years. I just hadn't noticed."

"You'd have had to develop other symptoms of syphilis in that time. You didn't get your deafness off a Dixie cup."

He had been healed of all his former afflictions. Unable to believe that in this age of commonplace medical miracles nothing could be done for this one, he consulted another specialist, although the first was famous in the field.

A friend had recently called him, the overnight expert, to announce that he too had gone deaf. He gave him the name of his first doctor. Remembering his friend's happy outcome, he said now to this one, "Are you sure it's not just wax?"

The doctor gave him a pitying smile.

As with all incurable ailments, having it diagnosed made it worse.

That he could hear people speak but not understand what they said began by seeming as though he were in a country where the language was English, but in a mode foreign to him. He had experienced that in rural Ireland, in the Bahamas, in parts of the deep South. But knowing that what he was not understanding was what he had always understood before brought sometimes a sense that what was failing was not his ears but his mind.

He seized upon his new hearing aids as Jude the Obscure did upon the Greek and Latin grammars, expecting them to provide a key, a rule, a prescription which would enable him to change at will all words of the dead languages into those of his own.

Jude was quickly disillusioned. "He learnt that there was no law of transmutation."

The dead languages had played a shabby trick on Jude, and he wished that he had never seen a book, that he might never see another one, wished he had never been born.

Had he found the key he was seeking Jude would still not have known how the dead languages sounded. Nobody now knew that.

He was not quite so naive as Jude. The purchase contract warned not to expect these devices to restore normal hearing. Well, eyeglasses did not restore your vision but they kept you from having to grope your way. Crutches were better than a wheelchair, dentures preferable to the alternative. But to be disappointed when your expectations were low was bitterness compounded. That disclaimer was an understatement.

Sounds reached him as though up the shaft from the bottom of a well. His own voice was distanced. He became a stranger to himself.

His sick jokes sickened him. Pointing to his ears, he said, "I've got AIDS." He said, "Now things can no longer go in one ear and out the other." And since they unselectively picked up all sounds in a room, he would say to the person seated next to him, "Let me take these things out and maybe I can hear you."

They were a nuisance. They fell out, got lost, consumed batteries. Ah, but when they began to fail him he felt marooned alone on a desert island watching his ship sail off without him into the infinite ocean.

The disclaimer accompanying the hearing aids warned also that they would not arrest the progress of the impairment.

His formula at first was a cheery "How's that?" or "Come again?" That sounded like what anybody might have said who had just missed a remark. As the silence thickened around him he said, "I'm sorry. Would you mind repeating?" Then like a bird limited to a single call, "What was that you said? What was that you said?" If others tired of hearing it they should know how tired of it he was! Finally, in discouragement, frustration, embarrassment, he gave up asking. Except of his poor long-suffering wife. He would have gone back to work so as to get himself out of the house but the only work he was fit for depended upon being able to hear. What kind of work did not?

He practiced lip-reading by watching television with the sound off. He was back with Jude again. He felt he had been sentenced to solitary confinement.

When in college he was first exposed to literature and decided he wanted to write, he set himself to memorizing the dictionary. He penciled the words he did not know. It was an absorbing assignment. He reveled in the richness of the language. He stuffed himself full as a fruitcake with long latinate words before realizing their uselessness and pruning his vocabulary. Now he was going through the dictionary again, this time crossing off the words he could no longer hear. In his second childhood he was unlearning to talk, going back to babble.

He knew now why in their portraits Beethoven and Goya looked so dour. Petrification of the ears gave to their faces an expression of stone. You could register no feeling when you did not know what was happening around you. Or much care, being no part of it. Music, laughter, words of wit, of love, the songs of birds, wind in the trees: all were lost on you.

"Go back off one noble size," his wife said.

Go back off one noble size?

"How's that again?"

"GO BACK OFF ONE NOBLE SIZE."

To foreigners, which was to say inferiors, who did not understand English you raised your voice and repeated yourself. "Oh!"

He wondered then whether he ought not instead to have said "Oh?" The interrogative rather than the exclamatory might have brought an explanation.

Later he learned that Gorbachev had won the Nobel Prize.

He whose first love was English now resented it for its teasing of him, its elusiveness. He remembered taking revenge upon French when on his first visit to the country his made him feel inadequate and uncultivated and he had sung, "I'm dancing with larmes in my yeux because the fille in my bras isn't vous."

Sometimes he thought he would go mad, and sometimes he thought he had. The unintelligible, almost intelligible babble in his head was maddening, was mad. He pressed his palms against his ears, creating a vacuum, then withdrew them sharply: a plumber's helper to unclog the drains. Unavailing. It would have been better, he thought in moments of obliquity, to be completely deaf, not tantalizingly half so, to have no memory of Mozart.

He had been a hunter, a bird hunter: grouse, woodcock. He loved watching the dogs range, loved the ripeness of the year, the comradeship. Now he no longer trusted himself to know at all times where his companion was. Out of sight of each other they hailed back and forth for safety's sake. He could not hear the dogs' bells, which meant he could not hear when they stopped tinkling as the dogs went on point. He could not hear a grouse take off when it was flushed — a sound to make a healthy man leap out of his skin.

He grew timid crossing streets, tires, motors, even horns being muffled, their distance from him uncertain. When driving he feared not hearing the shout of a child.

Well, but he could still write — that most solitary of occupations. He could were it not that in his sadness inspiration shunned him.

A kind friend gave him a book entitled *Adjustment to Adult Hearing Loss*. It was meant to comfort him. The consolation was in numbers. His wife read it.

"There are thirty million like you," she said.

"How's that?"

"THERE ARE THIRTY MILLION LIKE YOU."

"The dead are even more numerous," he said. "But knowing that must be cold comfort when you join them."

And if one more person said to him, "Well, it could be worse. You could be losing your eyesight," he would choke him.

At times he disbelieved it. It was a mistake. Any minute now it would clear up, like after swimming: the water would come gushing hot from his ears and he would hear again as always before. Or like after the plane had touched down and was taxiing to the terminal: one more swallow and then would come that welcome "pop."

Sometimes it seemed to him that he was just not listening attentively enough. He had almost understood what was said. If he just concentrated harder . . . Sometimes he persuaded himself that he *had* heard, only to learn that he had nodded in agreement when he ought instead to have shaken his head. Sometimes he felt he had not heard because he was so sure he was not going to.

All his waking hours now his head hummed with a trill like the treefrogs in spring, a sound he had always loved until it moved inside him. At other times the buzz was the same as static interference on the radio. *Tinnitus* that condition was called. Another label to have to bear.

Nature had made him deaf, he made himself dumb. As the

world receded from him he wrapped himself still deeper in silence. Hungry as he was for company, he avoided people. Their pity made him both pity and despise himself. The frustration they could not help showing sometimes after being asked to repeat themselves and still not being understood embarrassed him. His very expression of entreaty and anxiety provoked his wife. "Don't look so pained!" she said. "Don't listen with your mouth open." Then she regretted her impatience and was ashamed and he felt himself to blame for her self-reproach.

What should it matter that he could no longer follow the news on television? He could read it. But that was the very thing he could not do. The crackle of paper as the pages were turned, even the noise of a pack of cigarettes being ripped open, was excruciating, a sound like walking on sugar, amplified. If only he could hear other sounds as acutely as he heard those!

One dismal day his wife looked out a window and said, "Lots of cows up there."

"How's that?"

"LOTS OF COWS UP THERE."

"Where?"

"In the sky. Where else?"

"Cows in the sky?"

"CLOUDS! CLOUDS!" she shouted, and her shoulders sagged beneath the burden he had become.

As for him, he would have dashed himself against the rocks happily to have heard the sirens sing.

# The
# Parishioner

HER PASTOR, REVEREND SMITH, was being most supportive in Julia Johnson's bereavement. Her widowed mother's body was barely cold when he came to call. He came twice more before the burial. Julia was grateful, but after the third time she found herself rather hoping that he would not come again. Instead of better, his commiseration made her feel worse, instead of stronger, weaker. She was bearing up; he counseled her to break down. He encouraged her to let her tears flow, and he primed the pump. There was a time to mourn, he said.

Julia was sad but she was actually not quite so disconsolate as Reverend Smith told her she was, yet she could not very well disclaim it nor disappoint her comforter. For the truth was, she and her mother had not been every bit as close as he took for granted.

She must lean on him in her hour of need, being all alone, divorced, childless, with no brothers or sisters, said Reverend Smith. She had been trying not to think of that. Being reminded of it brought tears to her eyes.

When Reverend Smith said "lean on him" he meant it fully. The sight of her tears moved him to put his arms around his parishioner, lay her head on his shoulder, and pat her back paternally. He was by no means old enough to be her father, but he was taking the place of the one she did not have. She realized that her suffering had been deeper than she realized, wept freely, and felt elevated.

"You're very kind," she said, accepting the offer of his handkerchief.

"My duty, my dear."

At the funeral Reverend Smith eulogized the departed so fulsomely it made Julia appreciate her mother as never before, and reproach herself for not having done so. The pastor took as his text: "A virtuous woman who can find? For her price is above rubies. She spreadeth out her hand to the poor. She openeth her mouth with wisdom; And the law of kindness is on her tongue. Her children rise up, and call her blessed." He cited the dead woman's many good works in the community, generally unknown, for virtue blushed to be discovered. He spoke of her humility, her patience, her compassion. He dwelt at length upon her devotion to her late husband, to her only child. When he finished there was scarcely a dry eye in the congregation. All felt they had had a saint unnoticed in their midst. Behind her veil Julia wept unrestrainedly. Only now did she know that she had had the best of mothers. For this belated recognition she had Reverend Smith to thank. The depth of the regret he stirred in her made her feel she was atoning at least a little for her past neglect.

At the graveside Reverend Smith suggested that the mourners gathered around the hole all join hands in silent prayer. As the coffin was lowered to rest he gave Julia's several encouraging squeezes.

It was after the funeral that Julia's grief really hit her, as Reverend Smith had foretold it would. He was in steady attendance upon her at this critical time. How well he understood a daughter's love for her mother, the pain of losing her! The gravity of his bearing inspired confidence in his wisdom. His aptness with scripture indicated experience. He carried with him a spiritual prescription pad. His remedies were not sugar-coated. No false cheer, no shallow solace did he offer. He nursed her grief along, let it run its course, applied his sympathy to the sore spot like poultices to bring a boil to a head. He called daily, like a doctor on his rounds, took her emotional temperature, pulse and pressure. He had a most comforting bedside manner.

At last came the day when Reverend Smith pronounced that there was a time to cease from mourning. It was as though after a long illness her doctor said it had peaked and she would now begin to recover. Of course, convalescence would be slow. She had had a bad bout and had been left weak, shaken and susceptible. He was there for her to lean upon.

In the first phase Reverend Smith's text had been: "Let tears fall down over the dead. Weep bitterly and make great moan." Now from the same Biblical passage he drew this further bit: "Use lamentation, and that for a day or two, and then comfort thyself in thy heaviness. Thou shalt do the dead no good, but hurt thyself. When the dead is at rest, let remembrance rest.

"God's will be done.

"Amen."

In gratitude to her pastor Julia volunteered for church duties. She collected castoff clothes from donors, baked for fundraising suppers, visited the sick. She laid away her black clothes; however, lest it seem that her recovery had been too rapid, she still sought Reverend Smith's guidance as before. She assured him that, with his help, she was better, but he seemed to have misgivings about that, as though a relapse was to be feared. It was strange but true that his encouragement had the contrary effect of discouraging her. He made her feel that she was a person of deeper feelings than she knew, and for this she was grateful to him, but it also rather scared her and this made her more than ever dependent upon his support.

He was always ready with a comforting pat on the back, and one day with one lower down, accompanied by a kiss on the lips. They were alone together in the church basement's Nearly New Shop at the time. On their way to the couch in the vestry they passed the pulpit. The stained-glass windows shed their soft glow upon the proceedings.

In his sermons over the next several Sundays Reverend Smith inveighed against sins of the flesh. In condemning them he made them sound irresistibly tempting. Tributes to her femme-fatality Julia understood them to be. She felt flattered that her charms had lured a man of the cloth to dare perdition. Through her church activities she had made friends with Mrs. Smith, and seated in the pew beside her, she enjoyed the added luxury of pity.

"Powerful medicine, padre!" said parishioners to Reverend Smith standing at the portal to bid them godspeed as they exited to go home to Sunday dinner and afterwards to ruminate upon forbidden pleasures of yore.

# Last Words

Dear tom,

Many happy returns of the day. As the old song goes, "I gave you up. What more can I say?"

I read the announcement of your marriage in today's paper. It must have been a whirlwind romance. It is still less than a week since our divorce decree came through.

Your asking me for a divorce reminded me of your proposing to me. That time I gave you my answer at once, remember? So did I this time, though it was harder. But it was even harder on you, and my heart bled for you. The first time you had to convince me that you could support me, the second time that you could not, though neither time did I need much convincing. What worse blow to a man's pride than having to ask his wife for a divorce on the grounds that he could no longer support her but must ask her to declare herself a pauper and go on welfare? You need not have listed all the expenses I had incurred. The doctors' bills, the hospital stays, the costly medications. But it was such a painful step for you to propose that I understood your need to justify it. I regretted that I had not thought of it as a way out myself and spared you the humiliation of having to suggest it. It was not as though I never knew until then what a burden I had become.

You tried not to show it, of course, but I could see that my agreeing was a relief to you. It was to me too. I had done something helpful at last.

I once considered freeing you of me by doing what I am about to do now. I was prevented by the thought of how that would distress you, how you would blame yourself for it. I wish now that I had done it then. At least it would have been without this last taste of bitterness.

Goodbye,
Anne

# An Eye for
## an Eye

## *James*

I LEAVE HOME FOR WORK while the women are both still in bed. I leave early but by that time I will have done what many would consider half a day's work already. However little sleep I may have gotten I am up by five o'clock at the latest. I need no alarm clock. Not that I am eager to start the day but I am eager to end the night. Even on our better ones I am wakeful, expecting it to turn into another of the bad ones. On those nights I stay up throughout. I busy myself. While still in my pajamas I make my bed. When I have finished breakfast, bathed, shaved and dressed I empty the dishwasher, put the dishes back on the shelves. I sweep. I vacuum. I mop the kitchen floor. I water the houseplants. I do the laundry. The clothes are mostly mine, for the women, who never go out, live in their gowns and robes. I make a gallon thermos of coffee for them to find. It lasts them through the day. I set the breakfast table for them: cereal, cream, sugar, berries. I pack in paper bags two identical lunches: sandwiches, fruit, cookies. I might bake a cake. I take food from the freezer to thaw. I put together a casserole to be cooked for dinner. Once I could hardly make tea with a teabag but I have had to learn. I take out the garbage. I dust, wax,

polish. Although nobody but me, except for the occasional re-
pairman, has entered the place these six years, and although
only I have eyes to see it, I keep it as tidy and gleaming as if
company was expected any minute, God forbid!

Before leaving I walk the dog. There was a time when he
would never let me come near him, me nor anybody else except
his mistress. Would answer to nobody's call but hers. Bared his
teeth if anybody, including me, her husband, approached her.
He still does not like me, mutters and growls while I put on his
harness, but the tables are turned and now he is dependent upon
me. I never pet him but I am no longer afraid of him. Seeing
us, a stranger would think it was a blind man being led by his
seeing-eye dog. The truth is the other way round. I am the one
guiding him. We walk to the end of the next block and back.
That, twice a day — for I walk him again before bedtime — is
as much as he is up to anymore.

I could afford to retire. If I go on working the reason is not
that I enjoy it. I never have. I inherited the business. I have no
son or son-in-law, nobody at all, to leave it to, but I could sell
it, and for a good sum, for it is profitable. Not all the money in
the world could buy me out. The office gets me away from the
house for at least some hours of the day.

I keep a car but I use it only for shopping. I walk to work,
my only outdoor exercise these days except for tending the
grounds. Before, I used to play golf, but not since. I shot in
the low eighties. I liked to tee off early in the morning while
the dew was still on the ground. I played alone. With nobody
to see me I was tempted sometimes to pick up the ball from a
bad lie. I never did. Who would I have been fooling?

Our neighbors watch my passage down the street from behind their window curtains. People avoid me. Not because they
know the truth about me but out of consideration, respect. To

bid me good-day would be an impertinence. For the edification of all I hold my head high.

I know what they say about me because it is what I would say myself were I one of them.

"There goes poor Mr. Randolph. Poor soul! What a life! How he manages to carry on is a wonder. It was bad enough before, with just his wife, but after the accident to the other one — ! He could afford to put them both in a home to be cared for, or hire a nurse, a housekeeper, but no, he takes it all upon himself. And the other woman is not even related to him."

I take it all upon myself because I want nobody else in the house.

Many mornings on my way to work I make a stop at the post office or the branch library, sometimes both. I return the last book I borrowed and choose another, or rather, I never choose one, I just take the next one on the shelf. By mail, recorded books, a state service for the blind, go in and out of our house like the tides.

Once on my way downtown I pretended to be a Catholic. I had seen posted on the door of the church the hours of confession. I went toward the end of the time, hoping to be there alone after the other sinners had confessed and gone.

In the booth I whispered through the curtain, "Father, I have erred." I said "erred." I feared that I might not have used the right opening and have revealed that I was not a bona-fide member.

The voice asked me what my sin was, and, being unseen, I told. The priest must have heard a lot of stories not to be shocked at mine. So impersonal a tone came through to me that I wondered whether it might not be a recording. I had expected more individual treatment. He asked me if that was all I had to confess to. I felt like saying, "Isn't that enough!"

The priest assigned me a penance to do and told me to go and sin no more. I did not want to sin anymore, but the feeling of absolution I had hoped for did not come. I felt I had damned myself still further by my faked act of faith.

Mine is monotonous work. It both demands and dulls the mind. Eight, often nine hours of quotations, buy and sell orders. I am the last to leave the office at the end of the day. I am sure my employees say of my working late not that I am money-hungry but rather, "If I had what he's got to go home to I wouldn't be in any hurry either."

## Irene

It happened during one of the periods — the last that was to be (though the cause of that was possibly as much psychological as physical) — when I was in partial remission, always a bad time for me, for it raised hopes soon to be dashed. But a drowning person clutches at a straw, and at the start of that day I was grateful to be able to see even a little for however short a while, the way a soul in hell might be grateful for a moment out of the flames and prays it will last but knows the torment will resume and will be all the more painful for the temporary relief. Knowing it would not last, I never told either of the others. Why spread your disappointments?

The first time I ran to my doctor breathless with my news. Ursula was not yet with me then but already I had to have Rex, my guide dog. My sight was failing like the shortening of the days at the onset of winter. Or to put it another way, it was as though I had been taken captive and forced into exile and watched the shores of my world recede as I sailed away into the foggy and featureless void. Now the ship had unexpectedly turned back and brought me again in sight of home. Dim, to be sure, but discernible.

"Doctor, Doctor!" I can hear myself gushing still, "I'm better! I'm better!! It's a miracle!"

It was no miracle. As gently as he could, the doctor told me that it was in the nature of my ailment that these "remissions" would occur from time to time for a while. But the condition would progress, irreversibly. The coming night could not be pushed back. These were the last glimmerings in the dusk.

Thus I learned from one great disappointment to be thankful for another. How in my condition could I have raised a child?

I had longed for children with all my heart. In this big old house were rooms just waiting for them. We tried for them, my husband and I. We tried determinedly. We tried until the joy went out of the trying. As time passed, and with it, I feared, my desirability, I spent afternoons in beauty parlors, hairdressers' salons. From mail-order houses I bought undergarments that made me blush. But in my lust for motherhood I was shameless. Priestess of love, I made the boudoir my temple, the bed my altar. To make myself alluring I bought wigs, fishnet stockings, false eyelashes, Day-Glo lipstick. The savings account into which we deposited for the children's education was like a monthly offering to the god of fertility. I think my husband believed the fault was mine but all the same feared it might be his. I think that because it was, in reverse, my own feeling: guilt and blame, two sides of one coin — a loser whichever the toss. My fault or his, we lacked parenthood to draw us close, and there comes a time in married life, after the passions cool, when that is needed to sustain it.

I was lonely by myself in the house all day. I saw my husband off to work and wondered how to pass my time until his return.

The place was so neat there was nothing for me to do. I longed for the dirt and disorder of a large family.

Neighborhood children still played in the street outside our house then. This graveyard silence had not yet settled around us. I told myself I loved their shouts and laughter, for I feared that envy would be held against me in my hopes for one of my own.

In the course of the afternoon I would, in imagination, experience all the joys — even the tribulations — of motherhood. I nursed, I rocked, I crooned, I sang lullabies. I taught them their first words, their first steps. I cried.

When I missed my first period I trembled with hope, shook with dread. Was I about to fulfill my womanhood, or to lose it? Fearing disillusionment, I put off seeing the doctor. I yearned for morning sickness, outlandish cravings. Childbirth held no fears for me. I panted for the pain.

The story is told that a woman was ordered by her emperor to kill her mother and bring him the heart. On her way with it to the palace the woman stumbled and fell. The heart spoke and said, "Oh! Did you hurt yourself, my darling?" I would have been that kind of mother.

It was my misfortune, or so I thought at the time, to reach the change of life early. With conception no longer a possibility, my ardor cooled. We were considering adoption when my sight began to fail. Now if I have anything to be thankful for it is that there are no children in this house of horrors.

Instead of a child, I got a guide dog.

I was not only dependent on Rex, I felt beholden to him. He had been bred and raised to devote himself entirely to one person, in his case me, like a mate whose marriage was contracted for at birth, pledged to forsake all others, to love, honor and obey.

He was my servant, not my pet. He never frolicked, never nuzzled me, never licked my hand. He was as sober as a bishop. He kept others from me, he kept himself to himself. He and I were linked only by his harness.

His intelligence made him all but human. At once he knew our house from all others as surely as did the postman. He knew the red and the green of traffic lights, he skirted us around puddles, whenever there were steps to climb he led me to the rail. To just one command other than mine would he respond: that of a policeman who stopped the cars for us and signaled him to cross the street.

He slept at the foot of my bed — if he ever slept. I verily believe he knew when my eyes closed and when they reopened. Unlike a hunting dog, whose working hours are part-time, Rex was on duty around the clock, like a doctor on call.

But Rex was my eyes outdoors. He could not help me at the kitchen range, with pouring out the right amount of hot water, nor read to me the labels on medicine bottles, and doing such things myself got harder by the day.

Enter Ursula.

We advertised for a lady's companion. It was a serious step, to take in a stranger to share your home, your life. The first applicants we interviewed were all older women, widows, their children grown and gone away. They depressed me with their solemnity toward my affliction. Ursula alone among them was young. James said something that made her laugh, and that in itself was enough to win her the job.

We had a housekeeper who came twice a week, but Ursula took it upon herself to do the shopping, the laundry, and in the evenings she and James together cooked and served the dinner. I told her that these tasks were not required of her. She was to be a companion, not a housemaid. But what was she to do with herself all day, sit with her hands in her lap looking at me? I think that having grown up in an orphanage she was happy to have a house to run, in being its mistress.

As for her attentions to me, I could scarcely stir but what she was at my side. Actually, by that time I had learned to feel my way anywhere in the house. I knew the number of paces from one point to another and just when and in which way to turn. I had in my mind a map of it all from which I could have given directions. But Ursula so enjoyed making herself useful, having someone to care for, being appreciated. This too I think came in part from having been an orphan, with no one to lavish care upon. She adopted me.

I avoided people, not wanting my presence to dampen their spirits. Talk about my condition was carefully avoided, talk about anything else frivolous. My self-imposed isolation made me all the more grateful for Ursula's company. For James too it was a relief to come home in the evening to someone besides just me, someone bright and busy, cheerful.

But the young woman had no life of her own and I feared she would get lonely, bored, depressed at being shut in with an invalid all the time. I still went out occasionally, but while I had my Rex, she insisted on accompanying me. I could not refuse her company without hurting her feelings but I feared that my being with her would turn off any young person who might want to strike up a conversation, make friends with her.

In the afternoon she read to me. Recorded books were available for the blind and the service was free and efficient and in the evenings I listened to them through my earphones, but I liked a living voice and Ursula enjoyed the books along with me and that added to my enjoyment. We paused and discussed what we had read. We laughed together and we cried together. Our sessions began and ended with her saying, "Synopsis," and "To be continued."

The reading over, she drew my bath, and after that I napped — or pretended to. I urged her to go out by herself, go downtown, go shopping, see a matinee. I would have no need of her. I told her that our home was her home and that she must feel free to invite her friends there. She never did. I supposed she wanted to spare them the sight of me and to spare me being seen and pitied. I said, "When your guests come you will want to be alone with them, of course. I will go to my room while you entertain downstairs." Still she invited nobody. I supposed that she did not want them to see the confinement and narrowness of her life. At last I thought that as an orphan she had few friends or none. I felt that she was solitary by nature, or had been made so by her upbringing.

It was not, I am sure, to worm her way into my affections in order to secure a home for herself that she was so devoted to me. I was sure of that because she did not need to do so. She was soon made to feel like one of the family. It made the house more human to hear her hum and sing. She might be caged, but she was a canary.

After my nap she made me up. These attempts to maintain my "attractiveness" saddened me and I sometimes said, "Oh, what does it matter what I look like?" but she said, "Now, now. None of that. We must keep up our appearance."

One afternoon as she was penciling my eyebrows I yielded to an urge that had become an obsession with me. I reached out and lightly touched her face. She flinched, I felt it, and, already embarrassed by my impulse, feeling that I had taken a liberty and forced upon her an unwanted intimacy, I drew back my hand as from a flame. But she had recoiled simply out of surprise, not revulsion, for she instantly corrected herself and, taking my hand in hers, placed it on her forehead. Several times I ran my fingertips over her features. I felt a smooth, ample brow, large round eyes, a full mouth, a well-formed chin and a firm jawline, a shapely neck, rich hair. The patience with which she submitted to my examination declared to me that she felt she had nothing to fear from it, nothing to hide.

When I let her go I said, "Now I will be able to picture you in my mind. I know you better than before."

As the doctor had told me to expect, with the progress of my disease the remissions had grown fewer and further between and of shorter duration. Each might well be the last. So when I woke that Friday morning able for the first time in a long time to see a bit I did not cry and curse as I had done before. I determined to enjoy it for however long it lasted. Like a child at a fair, I would soak up sights. I would make for myself an album of images. They would be like souvenirs of a vacation. I would store them as on a roll of film, develop them later in the darkroom of my mind, linger lovingly over them forevermore.

For me the world that day was an art museum, rich in treasures. The house was a collection of dim-lit Dutch interiors. All out-of-doors was a gallery of Impressionist landscapes, the garden pond one of Monet's water lilies. So fresh was everything it was as though, seeing it for the last time, I was seeing it for the first time, and I was humbly thankful for my period of grace. All was out of focus, fuzzy, but perhaps the world was best seen when seen not too distinctly, in none too great detail. I let my faithful Rex feel no less necessary than ever, and with him at my side I spent much of that afternoon outdoors, going without my nap. Close my eyes for even a moment when I could see a last little something with them?

Flowers were in bloom. Roses! Snapdragons! Zinnias! Hollyhocks! I might have been Eve, before her expulsion from her garden, conferring their names upon them. Saying goodbye to them, I was preserving them, like pressing them in a book. For summer was on the wane and soon they would not be there for me not to see. They would fade and die as my sight would. But the bouquet my mind had gathered would remain as unchanged as a picture. And in the very impermanence of living things I now found a certain consolation, or if not consolation, some measure of acceptance of my lot.

That evening I sat alone in the living room, made up, combed and clothed by Ursula, waiting for James to come home. He was due any moment, and he was seldom late. His business was going well then and he was leaving the office at quitting time. I tried always to greet him cheerfully. I hated being the ball and chain I felt myself to be.

The sun was low, sending through the windows a horizontal beam like a trained searchlight. Too bright for even my poor partially restored vision. Like being dazzled by light on emerging from darkness.

James came in and thereupon Ursula entered the room.

For me to say that my eyes were opened then is no trite expression. Nor is it to say that I could not believe them.

She was naked.

Breathlessness alone kept me from gasping.

Like scissored cutouts silhouetted against the light the two embraced. Then she knelt, opened his trousers, reached inside, found what she was after, and —

I shut my eyes, but too late. They had seen more than I in my prayers had ever pled to see.

My first feeling was not one of outrage — that would follow. Mine was sickness of heart. Outrage and indignation were what any woman would have felt on discovering that this was going on in her own house. What so appalled me was that my condition should be a part of their pleasure. I felt deprived of my very self, treated as a thing.

Meanwhile, occupied as he was, James was saying, "Well, Irene, dear, how did your day go?"

I found my voice and managed to reply, "So far so-so. But it isn't over yet. Is it?"

He thought I was reminding him that this was a special day, one on our calendar. He was quick to say that he had not forgotten. I said sweetly that I was sure he would remember. I told him that he would find a bottle of champagne in the refrigerator. It had in fact been there for days. I had sent Ursula to the cellar for it. She had been puzzled to find the bottles not lying on their sides but standing on their heads. I said champagne was stored that way to keep the corks from drying and shrinking and letting the effervescence escape. She asked were we celebrating something and I said yes, but I did not say what.

Our wedding anniversary had passed unobserved. I was hurt by James's forgetting but perhaps not hurt as much as another woman would have been. Why should he want a reminder of being yoked to me?

I doubt he knew that evening that the date was wrong, he was engrossed in more immediate matters, but I believe she enjoyed the added zest to her wickedness in making a mockery of it, in, shall I say, pulling the wool over my eyes.

We toasted the occasion. The chill of the wine went to my veins, the bubbles to my brain. But it was not the wine that dizzied me. The change in my world was so sudden, so great, that for a time I lost all sense of who I was.

Seeing her sitting there in her brazenness I had a mad moment of thinking, well, maybe you are what is keeping my husband and me together. And what would I do without him? Or without you? The sense of my helplessness and dependency swept over me like a breaker.

We chatted. I was the most talkative. There was laughter. I

may have been the one who began it but their joining in sparked my fury. Behind my smile I said to myself, "Outrageous! You heartless fiends!"

Dressed as we were we dined *en famille*. James cut up my meat for me, and I forced myself to eat. I kept the conversation going quite gaily, thinking that they would enjoy their mischief all the more the bigger the fool I made of myself, and thereby earn for themselves the severest penalty. What was that to be? None I could think of seemed harsh enough to satisfy my bloodymindedness.

Our days, Ursula's and mine, were all so alike, so uneventful that we had little to recount to James in the evening. For us a call at the door by the Jehovah's Witnesses was an occasion. One staple of our dinner table conversation was our reading. Together we brought him up to date on the latest developments in our current book. We were then halfway through *Pride and Prejudice*. But rather than tell of Elizabeth Bennett's empty-headed sister's attraction to fatuous Mr. Collins I now said, "This being the day it is, I am reminded of the book we read not long ago. *Jane Eyre*. Remember? The last part, when Jane comes back and finds her Mr. Rochester blind and tells him she loves him now more than ever. There was a time when I would have scoffed at that. I would have said that only in Victorian novels are people so noble and self-sacrificing. You have taught me better, James. Praise to the face is open disgrace, I know, and I hope you are not blushing, but there comes a time when a full heart must speak out and give its thanks where due."

I then sighed and said, "The end of the book is unconvincing, I am afraid. Mr. Rochester regains the sight of his one eye and they live happily ever after. Now that does happen only in books."

James had earlier made a trip to the cellar.

"This," he now said, proud of his honoring of the day, "is Château Lafitte, 1982."

I was reminded of operatic trios, the characters singing conflicting sentiments but all orchestrated together. Said I to myself, "This is the grapes of wrath."

Into my mind came the phrase, "Justice is blind." I saw myself with the sword in my one hand, the scales in the other. But how in my condition was I to accomplish my revenge, one commensurate with the crime? James kept a loaded pistol in the drawer of his nightstand, but I was incapable of firing it even at point-blank range. Meanwhile, even as I considered, my eyesight was fading. With what was left of it I must act fast, before my personal night fell.

After dinner we returned to the living room. As I listened to the strains of Mozart through my earphones Ursula sat on James's lap, kicking her legs over the arm of the chair while he fondled her.

How in my helplessness was I to accomplish my revenge? It was just that, my condition, that came to my inspiration. I could hardly keep from crying aloud, "Eureka!" The very weapon I wanted was at hand. The one I would have chosen from among all others, given a choice. An eye for an eye! For what I was about to do I would need none. It seemed to me providential. Its availability set the seal of approval on my plans. I was being aided and abetted by the very gods of vengeance. I was their impersonal agent, with no choice but to carry out their orders. Humankind itself demanded justice for the crime done to one of its pitiful.

A short time before, one of the bathroom sinks had clogged up. So badly that none of the products advertised on television worked. From a plumbing supply store James got a bottle of something called Grand Slam. Concentrated sulfuric acid it was, so powerful that — although actually anybody could buy it over the counter — the label read, "For professional use only." The label said to wear goggles and rubber gloves while using it. A gas mask ought also to have been advised. It boiled and bubbled and hissed like a dragon in the drainpipe, and the vapors and fumes from it that filled the house were those of hell. It did the job.

James stored the half-empty bottle in the upstairs broom closet, not among other bottles, where it might have been mistaken, but in a spot all by itself, and he told me just where it was so I could tell the housekeeper not to go near it.

I was accustomed to finding my way in the dark. It was my element.

Her door stood open in expectation.

"James?" she purred. And that guided me like a missile to my mark.

## Ursula

Often at night I wake up screaming, and often I scream waking.

After graduation from school I stayed on at the orphanage for several years, tutoring the children. The pay was low but the place had been my only home. I knew I must move on, and I read the Help Wanted columns in the papers, but I had no special skills, and I feared the outside world. What I wanted to find was a live-in job. Appearances were against me. I was young, and I was not unattractive. The wives whose ads I answered did not want me in their homes. Then one day I saw an ad for a companion to a blind lady. I applied and was hired.

The lady was all but helpless. I found myself the mistress of the house. There was a cleaning woman who came twice a week but I did the shopping, the cooking. I read to her, chose her clothes, dressed her hair. It was being her companion that I disliked. She depressed me. At times I shut my eyes trying to feel what it was to be her. It was like holding my breath under water. Alive, yet doubly detached from the world as she knitted and listened to music through her earphones, she sat in her armchair as stiff as a statue in its niche. Seeing those skeins of yarn being turned into shawls and scarves I could not help thinking of a spider spinning its web. Sometimes I shuddered and said to myself, "There but for the grace of God go I."

In the evening after the dinner table had been cleared and the dishes put to wash we three settled down, she with her earphones on, the husband reading his newspaper, I with my book or magazine. There was a television set and she urged me to watch it but I seldom switched it on because she could not watch. And light entertainment seemed unsuited.

I would stifle a yawn and lift my eyes from the page and sometimes then I found him studying me over his paper. We both quickly looked down and resumed our reading. Between us there was some little awkwardness. It was as though she was not there, being both blind and, shut off by her earphones, deaf, and he and I were as good as alone together.

Then one evening in the kitchen he grabbed and kissed me. I was surprised at myself as much as at him. I did not resist nor protest. I felt a thrill at having attracted a man. Strongly enough to overcome his scruples. I, Cinderella in her chimney corner, had made a conquest — and the glass slipper fit. Never mind that I had not much competition.

He had seen in me something more than met the eye. He had shown me a side of myself that the mirror did not show. Of interest for the first time ever to another, I was instantly more interesting to myself. I had always been lonely, unloved. Placed as an infant in the care of paid guardians, strictly reared, dependent on the charity of strangers, I had had to be well behaved all my life. I was tired of being well behaved.

I now had a double life — I who until then had hardly had one to call my own.

I hardened my heart against her for what I was doing to her. The ease with which it could be done did not reproach me. Living with it as I did, I had come to hate infirmity, helplessness, dependency. Maybe my orphanage experiences conditioned me for that. I knew what it was to be both pitied and despised. Rather than appealing to my compassion, misfortune frightened me. It exposed the unforeseeable possibilities that lurked in life.

These are not excuses. Neither are they self-accusations. I have no need of either. My bad conscience, rather than making me repent, reform, goaded me on. I was trying to train it into submission, teach it that I was the mistress, it the dog, ordered to heel. That I can admit that now is the measure of how much I have paid for it. For what I did I deserved punishment, but not what I got. I have been more sinned against than sinning. I have more than atoned. I have been purged of remorse.

So we became a cozy little family. There was no reason that we should not live happily ever after.

But I was always nervous, ill-at-ease. Because her eyes were outwardly unimpaired I had to reassure myself constantly that she could not see us. Maybe it was partly to test that which made me more and more audacious.

Then there was that dog. I have since wondered whether it was not Rex who alerted her to the suspicion that something funny was going on. He was her eyes. The animal could do everything but talk, and his whole life was devoted to her protection. He was the fourth member of the family. He was as jealous of her as a lover, resented even my attentions to her. At anything out of the ordinary he bristled, and the telepathy between the two of them conveyed that to her.

Or maybe her suspicions had already been building before that evening, aroused by things I had said. I enjoyed saying things to her that had for me a double meaning. I had become perhaps reckless at that, skating on thin ice. I would say as I applied her lipstick, combed her hair, "We must look our best for our man. When he gets home from his day's work we must make things as inviting for him as possible. *N'est-ce pas?*"

I enjoyed also hearing her say things with meanings for me of which she herself was unaware.

"It's you who make things inviting. I can hear the difference in James's voice. I, too, am lighter-hearted thanks to you. I am so grateful to you for bringing light into this dark house. You do so much more than just your duty."

"It's my pleasure. Now then, what shall we wear this evening? Our purple paisley blouse and pleated white skirt?"

"Good. And you too, dear. I know it's dreary for you here, but make yourself decorative, for my sake."

"I'll do the best I can with what I've got to work with."

Had I overstepped myself? Had I allowed my tone in speaking to him in her presence to become unguarded, familiar, intimate? To any such inflection she would have been extra sensitive. When he and I left her alone to clean up the kitchen did she wonder what else we were doing as we did that? Did she, like any creature handicapped, feel herself vulnerable to attack?

Sometimes I thought she might not have minded if she had known. Sometimes I thought she *did* know, and that that was another reason for her appreciation of my putting myself out "beyond the call of duty." For they had separate bedrooms and when he left his it was to come to mine. There was something behind the way she sighed, "Poor James," that seemed to say she felt herself beholden to him for more than just her blindness. I came to feel I was doing her a favor, two favors. Keeping her man happy while relieving her of an unwanted duty.

As I had nowhere else to go on being discharged from the hospital, and had already concocted my story for the doctor, I was brought back here. It was where I would have chosen to go if I had had a choice. I did not fear any further harm from her. She had done her worst. She would want me here. And I was going to need a home, someone to take care of me from now on. In him I would have a devoted attendant.

The first time I ventured downstairs afterwards I got evidence for my suspicion that she had a sixth sense which only the blind could develop over time, hearing like radar to compensate for the loss of sight. She could have heard a kiss, the touch of two hands, the blink of an eye.

She joined me. I made not a sound. I hardly breathed. Yet, her voice aimed directly at me as though by an antenna, she said, "Is that you?"

I said, "What's left of me."

I rose from my chair, found my way to her, took her hand and placed it on my head. I wanted her to know just what she had done to me. At the same time I wanted to deny her the credit for it.

Her fingertips fluttered over the bald patches of my scalp, the pits and ridges of my face, the scars that were my eyes.

"Feel what I did to myself," I said.

I let that sink in.

"I mistook the bottle of acid James used to unclog the sink for shampoo."

It was what I had told the doctor.

She would be indebted to me for not denouncing her. Then

she would understand that I was not letting her off light. She would get no chance to defend herself, to expose my part in the affair. She would not serve out her sentence and then be let go. She would have me on her hands for the rest of my days. She would have to play along in the fiction of my "accident."

And he would come home to us both every evening and be turned to stone by the sight of me.

# A Tomb
# for the Living

WE WERE PLANTING POTATOES when the storm sprang up. What we were planting were potato skins. There was a better way to plant potatoes: in pieces, two eyes to a piece. But you did that only if you could afford to and if you had some hope that they were going to sprout. We had eaten the potatoes and we had no faith that these would come up. We were planting in dirt as dry as gunpowder and we had not even spit to water with. The well and the cistern and the stock pond were empty and we were hauling drinking water for ourselves and the mule. Nobody spoke anymore of a "dry spell." A spell could be short or long but not this long. As Pa said, speaking of rain, he was plumb prayed out.

This storm came on us so suddenly we had to run for it to the cellar. Or try to run, as we were heading into a northwest wind all the way from Kansas and it was like swimming against a flash flood. We had to close our eyes to keep from being blinded by the dust but you could not have seen anything with them open and besides, we had had to take to the cellar so often by then we could have found it in the dark. In years past we had sheltered there from the occasional cyclone, but in these years of the dust storms we spent almost as much time down there as we did in the house. The sound of the wind reached us through the ventilation pipe overhead like someone blowing across the mouth of a jug. It could be hours before it quieted down and we surfaced blinking at the light like prairie dogs.

Pa raised the double doors and held them while Ma and I went down the steps. There was headroom for me but Ma had to duck. We went always in fear of finding a rattler in there with us. We sat ourselves on the bench that ran around the wall. Pa lowered the doors behind him, shutting out what light there was.

When he quit coughing and gasping and hawking Pa said, "Lost my hat. Lost my goddamned hat."

He made it sound like the final blow.

"Don't take the Lord's name in vain," Ma said. "He hears you."

"He ain't heard nothing else I've said to Him," Pa said.

We sat silent for some while, coughing now and again. Then Pa said, "This is no way to live. This is hell on earth."

Yet the word that came back from those who had given up and gone west in search of a new life was to hold on if you could.

The way things were going we could not hold on much longer. We were not yet quite as bad off as some of our neighbors but we were only a step behind them. They were sharecroppers, we owned our land. At one time Pa had talked of selling out while we still could. But we had waited too long. As Pa said, we couldn't give the place away now.

Though the crops kept failing we went on trying. To plant this year's we had borrowed seed money. For Pa to be in debt was like having a noose around his neck.

Above the sound of the wind wailing in the pipe Pa said, "Like Onan, I have spilled my seed upon the ground, and the Lord has smitten me."

"Hush your dirty mouth!" Ma said. "For shame!"

"I'm only quoting scripture," Pa said.

A long time passed in silence.

"It's blowing to peel the paint off a house," Pa said.

"If a house was to have paint," Ma said.

It was still storming as hard as ever when Pa said, "I'm going out."

"What!" Ma cried. "Going out? In this weather?"

"I can't do what I've got to do in here," Pa said.

When he returned, he reported that the outhouse had been knocked to flinders.

Hunched in the darkness and silence of the cellar a person lost all sense of time. It was like being buried alive. None of us felt like talking. All we could think of was our troubles. At one point, even though the wind was then blowing its loudest, Pa could be heard groaning. Lately he was always shaking his head, as if disbelieving, and I had seen him often with tears in his eyes. Listening to the wind whistling in the pipe like a locomotive at a level crossing we knew that when we got aboveground we would again find the cornstalks leveled, the plowed land laid bare as a carcass skinned of its hide. This one might be no worse a storm than others before, but each took more of what little the others had left.

The wind blew and blew. It was hours before it died down, and it seemed longer. Even so we sat on for yet a while. We were in no hurry to have a look at the world after this.

At last Ma sighed and said, "Will, I reckon we can go out now." What she meant was she reckoned we had to.

Pa neither stirred nor spoke.

"Will?" Ma called again.

Still he gave no sign.

"He must have fallen asleep," Ma said. "Give him a shake, son."

I did, and he slipped from the bench to the floor.

I went up the steps and flung open the doors and let in the light.

Ma screamed and passed out.

Pa had cut his throat. His pocketknife lay open on the bench.

# Buck Fever

ONE MORE SEASON and then he would call it quits, hang his gun on the wall. This being his last, he was going for broke. The big buck or none.

The odds were long on none. That deer had become a lottery prize, growing bigger after each annual drawing without a winner — and attracting more bettors. For although hunters who had seen a trophy head of game did not spread the news in bars or clubs, over the years this one had been seen by enough to have a following dedicated to killing him. Deer like this one — if he had his like — were handed down from father to son, willed by friend to friend. The seasons passed with no report of his being killed. If and when that happened it would be news. Not just in the local paper but in the magazine published by the state conservation agency, in the annual review of the Boone and Crockett Club — just possibly in *The Guinness Book of Records*.

He had resolved at the end of last season that it would be his last. At his age it was time to quit, especially when you went for the whole two weeks without so much as aiming your gun. He had passed up a couple of long-range chances, ones he might have taken in younger years but not anymore. He wanted a sure shot, a clean kill—no trailing a wounded animal. It was not faith nor even hope, it was an obligation to stick it out to the end that kept him in place till dark on closing day.

It was that final hour when deer ventured out of hiding to move about, the time for the hunter to be most alert, but having in his mind now put his lifelong sport behind him he was inattentive. As the light waned and darkness fell it was as if the curtain was lowering on his farewell appearance. Already he was leafing through his scrapbook of memories.

If added proof was needed that the time had come for him to quit he got it. He woke from sleep barely in time to keep from falling out of the tree-stand twenty feet to the ground. Trudging home, tired, stiff, chilled, old, he was half glad that he had made no kill. He had neighbors to help him, as he helped them in return, but he was relieved not to be doing his share in dragging a carcass out of the woods.

Then as he entered the alfalfa field he saw the big buck silhouetted against the sky in the last glow of light. He saw two, both big. It was the comparison with the smaller one that was the measure of the bigger one's size.

He knew this deer. He had spotted him from time to time, usually out of season and always out of rifle range. He had found his hoofprints in the mud or in the snow and noted their growth like a parent recording a child's height on a wall. It had to be the same one, just as there was only one Mount Everest. Caution out of the common run for his kind had attained for the deer his prodigious size, his size had sharpened his caution. His extraordinariness was like a woman's beauty: a source of vanity and a constant threat. That rack of antlers on his head made it his crown and his crown of thorns.

By now the old deer must know as if he crossed off the days on a calendar when the hunting season was over and he could safely graze. He had come through now once again. He had won another year of life.

And the sight of him had given the old hunter another year of his sport — or had forced it upon him.

He did his homework more thoroughly than ever, for this time it was in preparation for final exams. Daily for two weeks before the opening of the season he was out scouting the territory: the pond, the woods, the fields, the abandoned orchard — his old stamping grounds along with the deer's: searching for clues like a sleuth on the scene of a crime. Deer were at all times wary, elusive, nearly nocturnal in their movements, still they had to eat, drink, sleep, and wherever they did they left their telltale traces. What most clearly gave them away was their reproductive urge, and their cycle brought the does in heat and the bucks in rut just before the hunting season.

The shortening of the days, the chilling of the nights, the hoar-frosts and the crusting of the ground, the rustle of leaves underfoot, the smell of fallen apples, the first light snows, the ice on puddles put geese in flight, squirrels to storing provisions against the siege of winter, and alerted deer to the onset of their yearly period of peril. The same changes in the seasons quickened his perceptions too, tested them, made him feel more keenly alive, a part of his world, which this time of year brought him most closely in touch with. That nip in the air was bracing.

Ordinarily he would have been pleased to discover that this was going to be a season with plenty of game. Among the stand of oaks, which had produced an unusually heavy crop of acorns, in the cornfield where, as part payment for the use of the land, his tenant farmer left standing the rows along the edges for the deer, he found signs in abundance. Now, instead of encouraging, these were a distraction from his single-minded pursuit, almost a nuisance, like pestiferous small fry taking a fisherman's bait.

But amidst all this he found what he was searching for. A

track as individual as a fingerprint. Other evidence in plenty as well. The old fellow was really living it up. Here he had lain in the grass. Here he had stamped. Here he had pawed. Here he had rubbed his antlers against a sapling, scraping off its bark, honing them for bouts with his rivals. You knew the sapling was his by its size: big. Here he had left his calling card for the does to scent, a yellow stain of his urine in the snow. The recklessness of his self-exposure almost suggested that after so long he had come to believe in his invulnerability. Or had he flung caution to the winds, sensing that this might be his last season too? Had he grown weary of his long reign, of disputing with the young bucks for his harem?

As D-day (for Deer-day), as he called it, neared the old excitement mounted in him as the rutting urge was doing at this same season in them. This time his was a bit sluggish. Coursing through old vessels the blood was slowed by some constriction. The drive had now to overcome shortness of breath, stiffness in the joints, but it was still there, and this he owed to the buck. The deer had given him another year, whatever the outcome of the contest between the two of them. It would have been wrong to say that he hardly cared what that outcome would be, but it would have been right to say that he did not care overmuch. He remembered reading that Winston Churchill, asked what he liked best of all to do, had replied that he liked best to win at gambling. Asked then what he liked second best to do, Churchill replied, to lose at gambling. So he felt about this high-stake game he was playing.

On the last day of the countdown he sighted in his rifle. His was not just an old one — that it had been when he bought it years ago; it was obsolete, already what was called a "wall-hanger." But if they didn't make them like that anymore the reason was not that better ones had replaced it. On the contrary; they couldn't make them like that anymore at a cost anybody could afford. Such hand-craftsmanship was long a thing of the past. Even its caliber was obsolete. Cartridges for it could not be had from sporting goods stores, only from one custom handloader out in Iowa. He now had left just six.

Hunters usually expended that many or more on sighting in. He fired one. Not only because he had so few; one was all that was needed for him and the gun to trust each other, to be ready for one last year together. The five that were then left would just fill the magazine.

That night before going to bed he laid out his hunting clothes: long underwear, the thick wool suit of red and black plaid with matching cap, boots, gloves, binoculars, sheath knife. He banked the fire. He noted with satisfaction that the barometer was falling. Who but hunters welcomed bad weather?

He would be up early, still deep in darkness, but he would need no alarm clock. Neither would the buck. Having heard the test-firing in the area all around today, that other old-timer knew as well as he did, if not better, what day tomorrow was.

In the night he needed more bedcovers and in the morning he woke to find the house an igloo. The temperature had plummeted. Even standing before the embers of last night's fire he shivered as he drew on his clothes. Another day and he would have been tempted to crawl back into bed, but today that shiver was electric. His battery was charging. It was as though, on a cold morning, hard to get started, his was attached by a cable to that of the big old buck. The weather was catering to his wishes. This hard frost would open the swamp, impenetrable at other times. Driven by hunting pressure all around, deer would take refuge there, in his own private preserve. And he had another reason for wanting to go now to the swamp. A sentimental reason. It was a fitting end to it all that he should spend his last opening day where he had spent his first.

He was in his tree-stand while still in darkness. He would have a wait of at least half an hour before daybreak. That would give the woods time to quiet down following his passage through them. Meanwhile his thoughts turned to that earlier day. He had been fourteen.

He had stood, not sat, and no cigar store Indian was ever more patient. Being on stand was like holding your breath for hours. Deer were color-blind but otherwise their senses were extra sharp. They were alert to the slightest untoward movement, the least sound, keen of smell. Itching all over, he forbade himself to scratch. Bursting to sneeze, he choked it. Chilled to the bone, he refrained from stamping his feet, flailing his arms. He tensed still further on hearing shots, for that stirred and scattered the deer. He had been warned by his father to be prepared to get buck fever if and when he saw one, and not to be ashamed of it if he did. Many an experienced hunter had frozen at the sight of a deer and been unable to pull the trigger. All the same he would have been mortified. He must make sure that what he was aiming at was a deer and not another hunter, and that it had horns. Should he kill one, his father told him, he would feel both proud and sorry. He must not be ashamed of that either.

All there was to remember of his first hunting season was having passed the test of enduring it, for although he was in the woods for two hours every day before and after school and all weekend he never got a shot. He was not disappointed; he had not expected to. He was not discouraged. It was big game he was after and he was a lowly apprentice. He was grateful for having missed none at least. It would have pleased his father if he had gotten one but it would have embarrassed him, for it would have been beginner's luck and he wanted to feel that he had paid his dues and earned his right to membership in the hunters' guild.

Now this day was dawning. The first light sketched in the woods, the rising sun brushed on the colors. On his spot game trails converged from all points like strands of a web, and at the web's center, motionless and tense as a spider waiting to pounce on prey that strayed into its circle, he sat looking and listening. The cold penetrated to his marrow.

He stayed until mid-morning, hearing shots all around — as many deer were probably killed on opening day as during the remainder of the season — but seeing nothing. With each shot he heard he prayed to Saint Hubert, patron of hunters, that it had not been the death of his buck. Out there were other men every bit as worthy and as dedicated as he. But prizes, as he well knew, did not always go to the deserving. The woods were also teeming today with tyros. What a mockery it would be should that deer, in an uncharacteristic moment of carelessness, fall victim to beginner's luck!

After breakfast he napped. In mid-afternoon he returned to his post and stayed until nightfall. He saw a herd of seven, all does. Silent as shadows, they filed in step across his field of view like a chorus line. Taking aim at each, he added them all to what he called his mental bag. He had long ago lost count of those.

On the third morning he woke to find that overnight four inches of snow had fallen. This called for a change in his tactics. The ground would be a sheet of paper covered with tracks as legible as letters. Everything that moved would leave its signature. The one he would be looking for was the John Hancock of deer. Rather than go on stand, today he would stalk. While waiting for daybreak he fueled himself with a big breakfast, and spiked his tea with brandy.

Deer had gamboled in the snowy fields like children out of school. But the tracks he sought were not among the many he found. No sun shone to tell the time by, but at what he judged to be around noon, weary after miles of trudging, he gave up. He felt somewhat shamefaced. Not because he had failed to find what he was looking for but because he had ever believed he would. He had been thinking about that one deer off and on all year long, planning his campaign against him, anticipating and forestalling his moves. It had become a bit like playing chess by mail. It had taught him respect for his opponent and raised his self-respect for being matched against so worthy a one. Now he had underrated them both. He should have known better than to suppose that that wise old soul would give himself away by cavorting in the snow like some giddy youngster. On nights like the one just past sensible creatures bedded down somewhere and slept late, assuming that even those intent on killing you had some sense too, and an appreciation of yours.

He plodded home, tossed down a jigger of whiskey and went to bed.

Tired as he still was, that inner alarm clock of his went off at the hour to issue forth again. As though covering his head with his pillow, he tried to ignore it. He felt disloyal to the hunter he had been since boyhood but now he had earned his rest. What was more, his inner barometer was forecasting another storm, and if his creaky old joints were right it was going to be a blue norther.

But if he knew that a storm was on the way the deer knew it better than he did. And that one he was after would in his wisdom take shelter from it in the pine grove.

Had that not been his father's aim in planting it? He had found deer inside it seeking relief from the heat and from the deerflies when the family went there to picnic on summer days and again on wintry ones when he was out hunting grouse. He had played peekaboo with them among the trunks. With its regular rows and squares it was like a chessboard and there he would have his opponent checkmated. On days such as this it offered an irresistible haven. The branches high overhead were so closely intertwined that rain, snow or sunshine could hardly come through, a canopy, and the fallen needles made a bed of the floor. He himself had often stretched out on them and dozed.

It was beginning to snow when he left the house. As yet you could count the flakes, but more, much more, was on the way. To the west, beyond the river valley, heavy clouds loomed above the mountaintops. A north wind was blowing, shaking last night's snow from the boughs of the hemlocks along the lane.

By the time he reached the hayfield where the long steep slope to the grove began he was puffing. He rested for a while, then drawing upon his second wind and shifting into low gear he plowed uphill.

He was soon forced to stop again. Panting and surveying the climb before him he wavered. He feared he was pushing himself beyond his strength. Meanwhile the weather was threatening. What he was doing was something for a young man, a voice told him. It was his own voice but it sounded only distantly like him. It sounded like a recording of him, saying nothing more than, "Testing. Testing." And he was spurred on by the thought that if he was tired, winded, he who had spent last night in a soft warm bed, well fed, he who was threatened by nobody, with nothing to fear, what must the deer's condition be? He felt challenged to a test of both his endurance and his hunting savvy. He slogged on.

Features of the landscape in the distance were growing indistinct, ghostly, those still farther away disappearing behind the advancing curtain of snow. It was as though his eyesight was dimming. Things were closing in. This land of his birth was as familiar as a womb, and the issue from it as assured, yet for a moment, shrouded in a sudden gust, sightless, he felt lost, trapped. To get safely home, he felt, would be like being delivered, swaddled, and put to nurse.

He pushed ahead, yet he would have turned back had he not soon thereafter found the tracks. No mistaking whose they were. They came up out of the swamp and headed toward the grove as straight as twin rails. It was as though he himself had laid them down. Self-satisfaction overrode his fatigue and his fears.

Halfway up the hill as he stood in his own tracks catching his breath there came over him a sense that he was being stalked, his footprints in the snow being followed as he was following the deer's. A sense that he, the hunter, was now the hunted. Irrational as that was, still more so was the notion that the deer had turned the tables and was luring him on.

He was still some fifty yards from the edge of the grove when the deer shot from it into the open. He dropped on one knee, brought the gun to his shoulder, pushed the safety off and swung the barrel for a long lead on his bounding target. Before he could fire, a pack of dogs, five of them, dashed from the woods in pursuit of the deer. With his first shot he brought down the leader, with his second another. The rest took off howling. By then the deer was out of range. He would not now have taken such unfair advantage of him anyway.

He experienced some unsteadiness in getting to his feet. He was trembling; his heart was pounding and he was short of breath. After all the excitement he needed a few minutes' rest. He went inside the grove and stretched himself out.

Weak though he was, a feeling of satisfaction filled him. He had read his adversary's wise and wary mind. He had foreseen his moves. The game was not yet to checkmate but he had brought it to check. He had the king on the run. And a king he was, even bigger than could be imagined, filling the landscape for that instant he was in the gunsights, and that rack on his head was a thicket of branches. Those two shots at the running dogs were surely the best of his life. He deserved congratulations for getting rid of those vermin. He felt a glow of charity in having spared the deer's life, and a sense of possession. That life was now owed to him. No doubt the deer too was resting somewhere at this moment, overtaxed and winded.

After a while the beating of his heart calmed and his breath grew regular. Still he allowed himself a few more minutes' rest. He would get home the sooner for it.

He was going to be tired when he got home. He could feel already how tired he was going to be. Tomorrow he would give both himself and the deer the day off. They had earned it. When he did get home this evening he would thaw himself out with a hot buttered rum and after dinner tuck in early.

Just thinking of that while watching the hypnotic snow sift down in this silence as deep as sleep made him drowsy. He must stir himself, get moving. He must not be caught out in this weather — or worse. Soon. Just a few more minutes . . .

Old Rip Van Winkle — whose haunts these were — did not wake from his long hunter's sleep to find the world more changed than he from his. He had a few moments of amnesia. The grove was walled in by falling snow. It was heavy enough to come through the thick treetops. He was covered with it from top to toe as though while he slept a sheet had been drawn over him.

He must get home!

He started to rise, gasped, and fell back unconscious.

There the body was found by the search team two days later following the biggest blizzard in modern memory.

# Ties of Blood

No two brothers were ever closer than Joe and I. The difference of four years in our ages made him look after me as if I was his child, especially after our mother's death, and made me look up to him with something akin to worship. For me my big brother could do no wrong.

Joe taught me to swim, to shoot, to drive. He helped me with my homework. He trained me in my trade. He could fix anything. Dad was handy, as a man has got to be around a farm, but Joe was a wizard. He could study a piece of machinery that he was seeing for the first time, and in minutes figure out how it was meant to work and what was now wrong with it. He kept the truck and the tractor running, the implements working. I never got to be the master mechanic Joe was, but whatever I know I owe to him.

When Dad remarried Joe felt himself to be in the new wife's way. It was time he left home and struck out on his own. He went to Dallas where he got a job as maintenance man in a plant. Dad was talking of selling the farm, so when Joe wrote saying there was work for me too at the plant I joined him. We set up house together. He worked nights, I worked days.

I took care of the same machines on my shift as Joe did on his. Between us we kept things humming. I might say, "Lathe number eleven seems to me to be spinning a little off center." And he, "I'll have a look at it this evening." At home we shared the cooking and the chores, and there too things went smoothly.

So did they after Gloria joined us. When I proposed and she accepted me I felt as if I had planted my flag on the moon. She gave up her job to become a housewife. Joe offered to move out but we would not hear of it. Gloria understood that he and I were inseparable. The two of them got along as well as she and I did.

The one thing that might have made me happier would have been for Joe to be as happy as I was. But as time passed I came to believe that he would never marry. All the more reason for him to stay with us. We were his family.

As soon as we learned that there was going to be an addition to it I said, "Joe, congratulations! You're going to be an uncle. If it's a boy he'll be called Joey."

Joe flushed with pleasure, and again offered to move out.

I told him this was his home.

One day shortly afterwards there was a power failure on my shift at the plant. Operations were shut down.

When I arrived home unexpectedly, I found my brother and my wife in bed together.

Had it been any other man I would have felt myself dishonored but I would not have been so hurt.

As I was loading the shotgun I heard Joe go out the back door. I spared Gloria, or rather, I spared her child. Which of us its father was I would never know, but in either case it was innocent.

Joe was waiting for me in the yard. To support my testimony he was still naked.

I said, "Joe, I idolized you."

I could barely see to shoot him for my tears.

# Auntie

I

"Miss rebecca" to all others, she was "Auntie" to just one. And as she was quick to point out on their being introduced to somebody, she was only Evan's great-aunt. Not that she wished to distance herself from him, as might have been supposed, but rather to account for the disparity in their ages. The villagers of course all knew the relationship. They had watched the Davis family drama played out on the street over the years. In his childhood they had pitied the boy. Who could help but pity the poor little waif, a runaway from the time he could toddle, seeing him being yanked by the ear or switched home by that mother of his, whimpering, humiliated before all the world, but still the picture of diminutive defiance? It pleased them to be able to pity her too, seeing that she had a heart to break after all. Even now, reading in the local paper of Evan's latest scrape with the law, they said, "Well, what do you expect?" But of her they said, some to her face, that she was a fool. Out of consideration, they refrained from saying an old fool.

On graduation from high school, head of her class, at age eighteen, she went to work in the local branch bank. She declined the honor of being the commencement valedictorian — the beginning of her reputation for being "different," one which escalated to the proportions of a scandal when, at twenty, on the death of her father, she left home and moved into the house next door, a rental property belonging to the family. There had been no quarrel between her and her mother and brother, she just wanted to be independent.

For forty years, immune to illnesses, she was at her post as surely as the flag outside the bank was raised and lowered daily on its staff. Indeed, because of her dependability, that task came to be entrusted to her. To nettle those who marveled at her constitution as though it were another of her oddities and who disapproved of old-maidenhood, she explained, "No husband, no kids to bring home bugs."

In all those years only one workday differed from the rest: the day the bank was held up.

Of the two tellers, the other one an elderly widow ripe for retirement, she was the one chosen by the robber. Sizing him up, she was not the least afraid of his deliberately using his pistol. Her only uneasiness came from his nervousness.

"That's as much as I can get under the grate," she said of the paper bag he had ordered her to fill with money. In fact, it was too much, as she had calculated. While he, having laid down his pistol on the countertop, tugged with both hands at the bag, she said, speaking low so as not to embarrass him, "Are you sure you want to do this, young man? They'll catch you sure as shootin' and clap you behind bars."

He gave her a startled look. Plainly she had said the very thing he was saying to himself. Leaving behind him the bag of money and his pistol, he bolted. He was arrested before the day was done, charged with attempted armed robbery.

She visited him in his cell at the county jail. At the time when they ought to have stood by him his family had disowned him. Customers at the bank wagged their heads and said, "Go visit the fellow who aimed a gun at you?"

At the trial she was the prosecution's chief witness. Having given the testimony that convicted the culprit, she pled the court for leniency on the grounds of his youth, his lack of a criminal record, and because "he had not gone through with it." Her unsolicited remarks were ordered stricken from the record.

Years later she received from Arizona a snapshot of the robber and his family and a note thanking her for having saved him at an early age from a career of crime.

She was credited with having risked her life to protect the bank depositors' money. A dinner was given in her honor, she was rewarded with a hundred dollars, and when the job fell vacant, was promoted from teller to loan consultant. Few borrowers ever defaulted on loans approved by her.

Banker's hours were short. Much of her time was her own. All the more reason for her to have a man to look after, said the village.

Her spinsterhood was held against her, as was her subscribing to magazines, which, there being no home delivery of mail, she was seen taking from her rental box in the Post Office. These contacts with the outer, alien and hostile world were suspicious; they might almost have been trafficking with the occult. She was too independent by half. Local boys were not good enough for Missy. Hoity-toi! She was known to have rejected two perfectly acceptable suitors in her twenties. One beau had come around to look her over as he might have hung over the fence to inspect a hunting hound or a head of stock. No more ardor did she expect, for so she thought most matches were made. The other fellow pestered her for a while with an attraction as one-sided as a fly's for a person. While both suitors seemed steady, neither inspired her to want to shop and cook for him, darn his socks, iron his shirts or share her bed and bathroom with him. "Love and marriage go together like a horse and carriage," said the song. As far as she could see, the wives were the horses and the husbands the carriages.

Her brother married and their parents thereupon retired to Florida. Over the following years the gate in the fence between the two houses stood open, but with the old folks gone and she with no children to play with their cousin, not much traffic passed through it. Her nephew, an only child, grew up, got married and brought home his bride, and her brother thereupon took early retirement, at a cut in his pension, and fled to Florida. Her nephew's wife was a gorgeous girl, the queen bee of the village, and might have had her pick of local men. She was said to have made the mismatch she had to spite the lover with whom she was quarreling.

She soon repented of her folly and she took out her discontent on her husband. Her voice was heard by the neighbors raised in anger; doors slammed, her car gunned off. The child that came did not bring with him harmony. It seemed that to his mother he only compounded her mistake. Miss Rebecca had another reason to bless her singleness.

One day while gardening she heard the child crying. On and on it went, until finally her concern overcame her reluctance and she went to investigate. He was alone in the house. She walked him until he quieted. She was returning him to his crib when her niece-in-law entered.

"He was crying," she said, feeling like a kidnapper caught in the act.

"They do that," said the young mother to the old maid.

On the way home she latched the garden gate behind her, and so it mostly stayed until the boy began to run away from home.

It was next door, to Auntie's house, that his first flight took him. No amount of exasperation could justify the mother's violence on retrieving him. She seemed to be taking out on their child her dissatisfaction with his father. The boy looked at his auntie tearfully and with a trembling lip.

Her maternal feelings were awakened as though by the angel of annunciation.

The mother cared about where the child was only when she did not know.

The little fugitive was not long in learning that his auntie's house was no safe haven. It was there that he was looked for first.

Fledged, he flew further from the nest, seeking refuge with the housewives of the village. They reported him by phone to his mother. He conceived a mistrust for the race of women.

From her window Miss Rebecca watched him yanked home, his mother loud in her denunciations, he unrepentant but suffering in silence so as not to draw attention to his humiliation. She knew that he would be the one to pay for her interference, and so she usually managed to restrain herself and, biting her lip, look on from behind her curtains, but sometimes the sight was too much for her and she dashed out for all the world to see, dressed as she was, uncombed, her hands clasped imploringly, and begged, "If you don't want him give him to me."

"Home! Get home! You brat, you!" the mother snapped, and she lashed the boy onward while he tried to protect his bottom with his hands, until they could stand no more and, sniveling, he sucked one and then the other to ease the pain. She felt the blows herself — as the mother had meant that she should.

As the boy grew and his stride lengthened and he ranged beyond his mother's reach, he passed beyond her concern. Her storming at him only made him more rebellious. She gave up on him. Once too strict, she was now too lax. She being the one who wore the pants in the family (for which the boy disrespected his father) he was turned loose. He was hardly ever at home. He began to run with a pack of local boys and was constantly in trouble.

Exasperated by both the boy's unruliness, his truancy and bad grades, and the parents' unconcern, the school officials threatened to take him from them and place him in a foster home. The father shrugged helplessly, the mother indifferently.

Because of this indifference Auntie's interference was no longer objected to. She was welcome to try her hand at reforming him. Trouble was, her pity for him made her excuse his misbehavior. What was to be expected of the child from a home like his? Temperamentally she sided with him against the authorities. In her own way she too was an outsider, a loner like him. Her halfhearted admonitions were ignored. He was not told that he was bad but that he had cause to be.

At seventeen — old enough to be tried as an adult offender — Evan was arrested as one of a ring charged with an epidemic of recent break-ins, convicted and sent to prison. He was hardly gone when, like a she-bear, which takes a new mate after her cub has been evicted from the den, his mother ran off with another man. The father went west and sank from sight.

When after four years Evan was released on probation, his auntie took him in to live with her.

## I I

To preserve her independence she had refused marriage. She wanted not to share her neat little nest. Not have to concern herself with another person's wants and ways. Not to wait hand

and foot on a man. Now in her old age she had invited disruption into her home, servitude into her life.

The villagers all smirked. Let them. They knew nothing about her that she herself did not know. She was as aware as they were of the irony of her situation, but she now knew the rewards of self-sacrifice and devotion, and the transfiguration that glowed about her like a halo wiped away the smirks.

Around the house Evan was idle, demanding, thankless, often moody. She excused him. He had had an unhappy life. He was untidy. This too she excused. At home he had gotten no training while in prison he had been harshly disciplined. To make up for this she let him sleep late on weekends, she made his bed, she picked up after him, washed his clothes, cooked for him tasty meals. Craving his affection and fearing his resentment, she refrained from criticizing him, from ever complaining. And indeed, happy to serve him, she harbored no complaints.

But about one thing she did nag him, for his own good, and this caused friction. She was worse than his mother had been in keeping tabs on him, in criticizing the company he kept.

He could not leave the house without her asking where he was going nor come back without her asking where he had been. "Out," was his surly answer to the first question, "Nowhere," to the second.

"Evan, you didn't get home until two in the morning."

"So?"

She lived in fear that he would violate his probation, the conditions of which were strict, and be taken from her and sent back to prison. She knew peace of mind only when he was at work, and she often phoned him on the job with such questions as, "What time can I expect you?" and, "What would you like for dinner?" to make sure he was there.

He resented the legal restrictions on his freedom of movement and association, the denial of his manhood. It was as if he were one of those wild animals, trapped then released with a radio attached to him to monitor his every moment. She pitied him and was pained to feel that he looked upon her as his jailer.

"Where were you last night, Evan?"

"At the Upshaws'."

The probation officer had called to check on his whereabouts. There had been some trouble in the area. She feared that if she were to say he was there with her he would be asked to come to the phone. It was to the Upshaws that she knew to go in search of him.

"What time were you there?"

"I was there all evening."

"You were not there when I was."

"Well, Auntie," he said impudently, "that's my story and I'm sticking with it."

And those Upshaws he consorted with would swear to it on a stack of Bibles.

She who had always been so self-sufficient and had never needed friends now solicited the sympathy of mere acquaintances: postal clerks, checkout women, mechanics, the new generation of tellers at the bank where she went to cash her pension checks.

"Here," she lamented, "is a young fellow. Well, so he made a few mistakes as a kid, but he's served time for that and now he's going straight, keeping his nose clean (she had picked up her jailhouse jargon from Evan), trying to make a fresh start. Still they watch over him every minute like guards. Any little two-bit break-in anywhere in the county and that probation officer is at the house grilling him. Car theft, arson, shoplifting — you name it, there's nothing but what he's number one on the suspect list. He's free to go to work but his free time isn't his. Can't have a friendly drink in a bar. Can't keep company with anybody who's ever had so much as a parking ticket. They keep him on a leash. It's not fair."

While some expressed a shallow sympathy, others, their patience with her plaint worn thin, told her that if, after a lifetime of freedom, she was saddled with these worries now in her old age, she had only herself to blame.

Some shook their heads in wonder and said, "Comes on like a choirboy."

It was true, for prison had taught him the benefits of good behavior, but it was not said as a compliment, rather as a comment on the deceptiveness of appearances.

He had inherited his mother's good looks, blond, blue-eyed, open-faced, and sitting across the table from him, delightedly watching him eat the appetizing things she had cooked, she wondered how he could possibly be suspected of any wrongdoing, or not forgiven if he had.

One Saturday morning while Evan was lolling about the house still in his pajamas and robe his probation officer arrived unannounced. The man had been there so many times that now he hardly bothered to knock at the door.

He opened his well-worn Evan casebook and prepared to take down the deposition.

"Where were you at half past ten last evening?" was his question. His look said, "This time I've got the goods on you."

Before Evan could frame a response his auntie said, "He was here with me. Straight home from work. We watched Buster Keaton on television and then put out the lights and went to bed at just half past ten."

She had been looking forward to an evening of popcorn and laughter with Evan. She had watched Buster Keaton alone.

The probation officer, a local boy, closed his book.

"If you say so, Miss Rebecca, I believe it," he said.

Corrupted by love, she had sacrificed a long lifetime of honesty.

When the officer was gone, she said to Evan, who was unable to look her in the face, "Now then. Where were you? You can tell me. I have a right to know. Now."

# Vissi d'Arte

It was saturday evening. Fun day in the Big Apple. People were returning home at the end of an afternoon of shopping, gallery-going, matinees, exhibitions. It was raining. The only way to have stopped a taxi in mid-Manhattan would have been with a shot. He stood in the flooded street trying to hail one with a hand raised like that of an overlooked auction bidder while Jane sheltered beneath her umbrella on the curb. Behind her a man was trying to steady himself against the wall while taking a shit. The place he had picked, consciously or not, was especially well suited to his purpose, for on the wall in artistic lettering was sprayed, SHIT PISS FUCK NIGGER KIKE WOP.

The changing of the stoplight down the avenue from red to green released the stampeding herd of traffic as from a pen. Between times he joined Jane. He was worried more even than usual at this hour over her. She looked so forlorn! In further-ance of her career, they too had done their Saturday gallery-going, always an ordeal but this time devastating.

"Well, Jane, dear," he said soothingly, "it's nothing new. We've been through it before."

But today was something new, a turning point, not just more of the same. He, her weeklong art patron, her weekend agent, he their font of faith, had crumbled and had disclosed to them the depth of their desperation.

The day had begun unexceptionally, promising to be nothing worse than their usual weekly draught of wormwood and gall. He breakfasted as always on Saturday on sour grapes, that was to say on the art-show reviews in the Friday edition of the *New York Times*. This he did so as to fortify himself against the snubs and brushoffs awaiting them and to scoff at the trendy world they wooed.

He finished his reading and made like a chimpanzee with his lip and forefinger. Crumpling the paper, he commented, "Wrap tomorrow's fish." Then, "With today's painting if you're not insulted you've missed the point. The situation has brought me to side with Herman Goering: 'When I hear the word *culture* I reach for my pistol.'"

From his notebook containing page after page of crossed-out names of art galleries he read aloud those on today's list. Then, color slides in their box, earplugs in place, and after a brief delay on the stoop for the neighborhood thief on his daily rounds to finish ransacking the pockets of the derelicts sleeping there and, finding nothing on any of them, to give the last one searched a kicking for them all, they set forth once again to encounter Saturday and the art world. They were stopped by a young panhandler on the street just long enough for a bill to change hands. It was not necessary to unplug an ear to know that he had said, "Let me hold five for you, buddy."

By now refusal could take no form not known to them.

"Thank you." (This after a perfunctory glance at half a dozen of the slides.) "Interesting, but not for us, I'm afraid. Now if you will excuse me . . ."

Or:

"Sorry, but we are not able to take on any new artists at this time."

Or:

"We're booked up with shows for years to come."

"But don't you even want to look at the slides?"

"Sorry. Now if you will excuse me . . ."

He always crowned their Saturday with a visit to one or another of the big-time international galleries. So often had they been to some of them that they were known there by name. She felt this was a waste of time; he did not feel it was a waste of time, he knew it was. She felt it was humiliating to be turned away again and again by the same people. He felt those people were storing up humiliation for themselves. When discovery caught up with her, and the question was asked on all sides, why had it taken so long, they would be flushed from their corners by the searchlight of revelation and stand naked, blinking and stammering in the glare.

His reading was all but confined now to the biographies of artists. It was like for a Catholic the lives of the saints and martyrs. Van Gogh's lack of funds for a postage stamp to send his brother one of those precious letters of his, poor Pissarro's struggles to feed his large family, Sisley dying of malnutrition only to begin selling for thousands while still warm in his grave: all this sustained and uplifted him. Her time would come. Meanwhile, crossing off each gallery in his notebook added another notch to his gunstock.

Not for a moment did he believe that his persistence would wear down or enlighten these art establishment mafiosi. A survey of the smears and daubs on their walls was enough to convince him that they were beyond redemption. It was not their acceptance he sought, it was their unwitting self-condemnation. He relished their fatuous superiority, almost twitched with glee when one of them said, after glancing at the slides, "Not for us, I'm afraid."

"Not for you."

"I'm afraid not."

"You're afraid not."

"Afraid not."

"Well, Jane," he sighed, "looks like you'll have to go on starving in your garret for a while yet."

He jigged in the street afterwards and sang, "So we'll put them on the list and they never will be missed. No, they never will be missed. No, they never will be missed."

On the sidewalks of New York no nut was noticed.

Sometimes he fantasized having one of these *machers* suddenly see the light, say, "Where have I been all this while? Why, these are marvelous! A whole new vision! Just what the world is waiting for! We'll show them," and he gathering up the slides and saying, "You'll lick spit before we let you have them. Come, Jane."

After one of these interviews he would say to her, "I wouldn't want you to be represented by those people."

There was a time when she had agreed, but now if she said anything it was a wistful, "I wouldn't mind."

Now on this day in late afternoon she plucked at his sleeve. To hear what she had to say he steered them into a store, for in addition to the pounding of tires in potholes and the rattle of vans a woman was crying, "Shithead motherfuckers," as though she were vending them.

When he had removed an earplug Jane said, "Allen, let's not go to the Melrose today. I'm so tired. And it will only be the same as always."

"Oh, yes! We most certainly are going to the Melrose. It's their turn. Of course it will be the same as always. That's the point."

It would go like this:

"But, Mr. Sanford, Ms. Randall (her professional name), we have seen your slides." (Sigh.) "Many times."

"Not these latest ones, you haven't."

"Sorry."

"How do you know you're not overlooking the next Cézanne?"

"Ah, yes." (Sigh.) "Every dealer's nightmare. Chance one must take, I'm afraid. One of the risks of the trade. Now if you will excuse me . . ."

These days, what with the astronomical rise in art values — and the consequent rise in thefts — you did not just walk into a picture gallery from off the street. Not those where the likes of Jasper Johns were hung. You rang for admission, and through the thick glass door you were inspected before what he called the Sesame button was pressed. It had not yet gotten to speakeasy ways; you did not have to say through a peephole, "Joe sent me"; you had only to look respectable, or if not respectable, rich. Any art thief with the braces off his teeth would have gotten past this barrier by dressing himself out of Dunhill's, renting a Rolls-Royce and having his liveried chauffeur and accomplice double-park it as though immune to meter maids and traffic tickets.

The Melrose Gallery stood high on his hit list and he hit it often. With branches in Dallas, London, Paris, Tokyo, a trend-setter, a weathervane in the winds of artistic fad, it represented all that he despised. Having rung the bell, they stood at the door to be recognized by their old friends Messrs. Taylor and James, the directors. He gave them his gallery smile and his little bow.

He rang again. Still the buzzer did not sound. He rang again. He could see the two men clearly and could see that they saw him, that in fact they were discussing him. He could almost read their lips, he could certainly read their expressions.

The accumulated spleen of years rose in him like a clogged drain regurgitating. He beat with his fist on the door.

"Yes!" he shouted. "That's right! It's 'those two' again! Open up!"

He set down the box of slides and, shaking with outrage, pounded with both fists. The door remained locked.

"You dirty bastards!" he shouted. "You charlatans! You pimps! You supercilious shits! Who do you think you are? Who appointed you to decide what is art, you crappers?"

It was not the sight of one of them dialing the phone for help that silenced him, nor was it any embarrassment over the public spectacle he had made of himself. He was shaking now not with indignation but from fright at his outburst. Not defiance but defeat was what he had exhibited. He had revealed to himself and to Jane the futility of their long quest.

Plodding the thirty blocks home after giving up on getting a taxi, fearful of breaking the silence by saying anything, he said only, "Well, Jane, you're in good company."

Having heard that too many times before, she said nothing.

The next day, Sunday, while Jane went to her studio, he prepared for his annual income tax audit. It was the prospect of this that had contributed to his outburst of the day before. As with chips on a gambling table, he stacked the receipts for the studio rent, canceled checks for models, for the photographer who came monthly to take the color slides. In francs the bills from Lefebure, the Parisian color merchants with whom she had a charge account — last remaining source of broad red sable brushes — ran off the page. Converted by calculator into dollars, the figure was still fingerlength. Not only was she undaunted by the world's rejection, she defied it. She was challenged to produce even more. Her courage in the face of adversity, her unsparing dedication to her art was a wonder and an inspiration to him. Six days a week, with Saturdays off to make their rounds of the galleries, she was in her studio and at her easel from nine in the morning until six in the evening. (They dined out.) She had held her babies in one arm while she painted. Her prodigious output was proof in itself of her genius. Not even Picasso was more fecund. How could he be disheartened when she was so steadfast? He must be the Théo to her Vincent. Like Philip IV with Velázquez, he was honored to pick up her paintbrush when she dropped it. Yet though pity for himself made him feel disloyal to her and to their common cause, he could not help uttering a plaintive, "Vissi d'arte." He followed it with Tosca's, "e d'amor." And even so, he dared not claim her full expenses for fear of being disallowed them all. That threat had hung over him for years like the blade of a guillotine.

Time was when he had had to undergo not one but two annual audits, the first in rehearsal for the second, like being crammed by a tutor for an exam. This was with his accountant. Charley's patience with him had worn almost as thin as that of the Internal Revenue Service.

"All that imported Belgian linen canvas!" Charley lamented. "Those expensive Block colors! Does she have to paint so *big?*"

This stung him because he had once timidly ventured the same question himself, when the storage bill for the nine hundred canvases in the warehouse in Yonkers reached four figures. Perhaps, he suggested to her, gallery owners were put off by their size. Most apartment-dwellers did not have that much wall space. This was met with the scorn it merited. She was not painting pictures the size of doily cloths like those to be bought at supermarkets. Did Monet think of petit-bourgeois *locataires* when doing his water lilies? Did — though in no other respect would she ever compare herself with them — did Pollack have in mind mobile homes, or Stella? Her eyes were set on the dimensions of the Marlborough Gallery, the Museum of Modern Art. Even they — the snots! — would see the light in time — or if not in time, in time to come. Then she would have her vindication! Meanwhile in defiance she painted more and more monumentally.

"Look, Al," said Charley, "you're in a position now where you could afford to retire if you sold out and got out of the city and away from these ruinous expenses. You hate it here anyway."

"You don't understand the art world, Charley. Here," he said, quoting Jane, "is where it's at."

"This may be where it's at but you're still knocking on the door."

This sort of thing he had to put up with from the IRS. Did he have to pay for it too?

"Move up to Woodstock. How long is it since you went fishing? Woodstock: that's the ideal place for both your interests. It's an artists' colony. There's art all over the place. In banks, cafés. Up there she might even get a show in one of the local galleries."

He shuddered to think of Jane's reaction to the suggestion of a show in some "local" small-town gallery.

"For not much more than you're paying in yearly rent on the apartment and the studio you could make a down payment on a home up there. A nice old farmhouse. Hell, you could get a place with a barn big enough even to store all Jane's . . . stuff."

It was that "stuff," and the pause preceding it, that cost Charley his longtime job.

Shy of having another accountant see into his private affairs, he now prepared his tax return himself, and went unaccompanied by counsel to his annual audit.

\*

"According to our records," said the IRS official, "it is now —— years that you have been claiming business expense deductions for your wife's painting." As on television when someone uttered an obscenity, his mind had blipped out the number. "In all that period of time just four pictures have been sold."

Actually they had not. He had falsified those sales, thereby diminishing his claim, in hopes of making it look as if her efforts to sell were earnest.

"We do not insist that a business show a profit every year," the man continued. "But the government can no longer subsidize you in what is, we submit, a hobby. An expensive hobby."

Had Jane heard that she would have choked with indignation. Shades of Cézanne! Holy Vincent!

Onto the screen of his mind flashed a set of figures:

| | | |
|---|---|---|
| Item: | "Portrait of Dr. Gachet" | |
| Income: | $82,500,000.00 | |
| Expenses: | canvas | $20.00 |
| | Paint | $10.00 |
| | Studio rent (1 hr.) | $1.00 |
| | | $31.00 |
| Net profit: | $82,499,069.00 | |

"Your deductions are disallowed."

Although this was what he had anticipated with dread for years, and more with each year, it came nonetheless as a blow. Without those allowances there was no way for him to make ends meet.

Shaking his head incredulously, as though dealing with someone deluded, the IRS man had read off the figures for the studio rent, the supplies, the models, the storage bill on the nine hundred pictures in Yonkers, etc. Each wove a strand in the web he was tangled in like one of those hapless insects injected with anesthesia by its captor and slowly sucked dry of its juices.

A sensation as though he were grappling with an octopus assailed him as he waited for the elevator in her studio building. When he opened her door, fearful that his disloyal thoughts might have left telltale traces on his face, he eased himself out without being seen. She was on a stepladder working on her current canvas. Hobby! He likened her heroism to that of Michelangelo lying on the scaffold and painting over his head for ten years.

Without telling Jane, he took a day off from work and, slides in hand, made his own round of galleries. New ones opened weekly in the SoHo district — and just as often closed. It was both of these factors he was counting on now, for in this lone foray of his he had in mind an opposite approach from their usual one. Turned away repeatedly at the front door, he was going now to try the back one. Jane would die of shame if she knew what he was up to, would disavow him, would divorce him, but he was desperate. The ruling of the IRS to disallow his deductions for her was not his only worry. The other was his mounting concern over her. As though he had a thermometer and a chart at the foot of her bed, he could see that her fever was peaking. It was not that she was painting any less determinedly than before. On the contrary. What was alarming was that she was painting with both hands, like a mariner trying to bail out a sinking boat.

The reception he got at the first place he tried shook him so thoroughly he shied from repeating it at the next one.

The lady owner of the gallery was replacing the few slides she had glanced at, preparing — he could hear it coming — to utter the standard, "Sorry. Not for us," when he propositioned her.

"Where do you think you are?" she demanded indignantly.

"This is a reputable establishment, I'll have you know! We are not for hire. Good-day to you, sir."

At Pettingill et Cie he began his pitch, "My wife is an artist."

*Whose isn't?* said Mr. Pettingill's weary expression.

"May I show you some color slides of her work?"

Like the lady at the first gallery, Mr. Pettingill seemed to wonder where he thought he was, only with a difference. One for not beating about the bush, Mr. Pettingill said, "That won't be necessary."

Though this was what he was after, he disbelieved for a moment that he had found it, or that it could be so blatant, so unashamed. In the silence that ensued they took each other's measure. Mr. Pettingill named his price. It was breathtaking. This was no lottery. This was more like buying the prize in hopes of winning the ticket.

The following Saturday, as always, before setting off on their rounds, he read aloud the list of the day's galleries. The Pettingill was the last. He planned to produce Mr. Pettingill at the end of another dreary Saturday like a rainbow.

"Have we tried any of those places before?" she asked.

"No. All virgin territory."

She did not rise to his chirpiness. Even as he read them aloud she could see those names scratched through like all the others in the book.

In early afternoon, with three down and one more to go he could see coming on that tightness around her lips and that furrow between her brows that signaled discouragement, and he decided to go directly to Mr. Pettingill.

"Well, Jane, dear," he said afterwards, "it's not the Melrose, but it's a start."

"Now don't go putting down my gallery," she said. "Oh, wasn't Mr. Pettingill wonderful! So enthusiastic!"

Yes, Pettingill had played his practiced part in the charade smoothly, and had looked to him for appreciation. He had felt like one of the countless customers of a well-worn whore.

"So *perceptive!* He understood my aims entirely. I could see that you were a bit annoyed at his pointing out my influences, but I didn't mind a bit. I have always gratefully acknowledged my debt to the masters. Oh, Allen, this has been a long time in coming. Without you to keep me going I could never have held out for so long. I am so grateful to you for your loyalty and faith. I do hope you feel now that it has all been worth it. Oh, what a difference a day makes! I'm a new woman. I'm so happy I could cry, and I believe I'm going to."

The end would justify the means. The ads he had placed in the *Times* and the *Village Voice* would draw viewers to the show. The papers would send their critics. Nowadays, to hedge against the future, not knowing what they liked anyway and with no standards to guide them, collectors and curators were afraid *not* to buy pictures. Other, honest galleries would woo her. In time the museums would take notice and there would be a retrospective. Those canvases, some anyway, could come out of storage in Yonkers. In the meantime, he could return to the IRS with proof that hers was a serious, professional, profit-seeking enterprise, not a "hobby."

Had he really believed all that? Now that it had not happened he could not believe he had, but before it had not happened he had believed it would.

They chose the pictures to be hung and together drew up a list of prices for them. Her expectations seemed unrealistic even to him.

"They're worth every bit you're asking, and more," he began by saying. Then after a pause, "However, we must not forget that your reputation has yet to be established. What you want is for the pictures to find homes. Let people see them on their friends' walls. Spread the word. Perhaps if the prices were a bit more attractive . . ."

"Hold yourself cheap and so will the world," she said.

She wanted to be present at the gallery throughout the duration of the show, surrounded by her productions, watch people look at them and overhear their admiring remarks. Mr. Pettingill was glad to let her mind the store. He gave her the key and went off on vacation.

The pictures were priced on request. As the days passed the prices were revised downward. "Hopscotch" had originally been $5000; now she would entertain an offer of $3500. Appreciative people could have "Rope-Jumping" for $2500.

During the two weeks the show hung some two dozen visitors came to the gallery. They looked as though they were lost and had wandered in by mistake. They left hurriedly. A few others poked their heads inside and withdrew them as though they had smelled a bad smell. Sitting there she felt, she said, like the lady attendant of a Paris pissoir. She had begun like a bouquet; like a bouquet she wilted more daily.

Mr. Pettingill returned from his vacation on the closing day of the show to supervise the taking down of the pictures. They were stood with their faces to the wall like punished school-children. In their places those of the next show were hung without delay. Mr. Pettingill's bed was never allowed to cool.

Now it was the morning of the day after.

It was no time to be thinking about fishing, but fishing was what he was thinking about.

He saw himself stepping into a landscape by an artist of the Hudson River School: Thomas Cole, Frederic Church, George Innes — misty, silent, still. Time had been turned back to the sixth day of its creation and he was the first person on the scene. While in the city streets outside the studio where they sat waiting sirens wailed like wolves, in his fancied world trouble was as yet unknown.

He waded knee-deep in his favorite stretch of the Catskills' Willowemoc. The headwaters of that stream rose in heaven, and there it was stocked with trout.

To choose from among his flyrods — the Garrison? the Halstead? one of the Paynes? — was always hard, each had its memories, but you could fish with only one at a time, and, precious though it was, its worth measured in karats, today he had chosen the seven-and-a-half-foot "Pinky" Gillum. It was just as well that for the past several years he had fished only in fantasy. Split bamboo rods were delicate, breakable, and though he was no longer an active member of the fishing fraternity, word had reached him, if from no other source than the *Wall Street Journal*, of the spectacular appreciation in the value of such "classic" rods as his, crafted by makers whose like would not be seen again. Even so, he was unprepared for the sum they fetched when he auctioned them to help pay Mr. Pettingill. Having no use for them anyway, his weekends being otherwise occupied, he had kept his in guarded and bonded storage. When Jane achieved recognition, a lasting gallery connection, and his Saturdays were his again, he would go back to fishing. Occasionally he sneaked a visit to the warehouse and while nobody was looking jointed a rod and flexed it. He felt then like a conductor with a chorus of trout at the bidding of his baton. For in all modesty, he had made of himself a maestro. If, as the brothers of the angle liked to think, time spent fishing earned you time off in purgatory, then for his early years he ought to have been whisked right through.

It was just sunrise with steam hovering above the water.

So silent was the world that he could hear the big fish rising greedily, unguardedly to a hatch of insects — Hendricksons they were, size 16 — forty feet upstream of him. He presented his fly just above and to the left of the fish for it to float down to him on the current. He tensed for the strike . . .

"Here they are," said Jane.

They looked out the studio window. Down on the street two men inside the moving van were handing the pictures to two outside.

He was about to say, "Well, dear, you're in good company," but he was silenced by the look on her face of fixed dejection.

# Virgin
## and Child

On the nights when she attended evening classes Cecily stayed over with her uncle and aunt in Manhattan rather than return home to Brooklyn. Danger lurked in the dark streets; the subway was a sewer. A lone young woman had to dart from cover to cover like a head of game. Cecily's defense was to make herself drab. No makeup, no jewelry, shapeless sweaters, loose long skirts, flat heels. She looked like Garbo off the lot.

But just as Garbo could not turn herself into a scarecrow so Cecily's camouflage did not mislead every predator. One had approached her minutes earlier as she was trying to hail a taxi. She looked through him, nodded as he spoke and, smiling charitably, handed him a dollar. He was so nonplussed he took it. She left him looking put down as her taxi pulled away.

Cecily's uncle and aunt lived in a neighborhood as desirable as could be found in the city these days. The doorman of the building, whom she called "Saint Peter," let her in. She pressed the elevator's Penthouse button and in sixty seconds made an ascent as full of contrast as Dante's climb from Inferno to Paradise.

The penthouse transported you in time as well as place. It was Early Hollywood, suitable as the set for a Fred Astaire film. The decor was Art Deco, that elegant artificial style designed to deny the grim reality of its period. High in the sky, insulated from the city's din and squalor, you imagined top-hat and tails, dancing cheek to cheek, the pop of a champagne cork and the kiss of glasses. Her uncle, pleased with himself and with his rise in the world, once looked out the big picture window and said, "We're on Cloud Nine."

This evening, with Cecily to baby-sit for them, her uncle and aunt were going out to dinner and the opera. The production was Wagner, so they would not get home until morning. Cecily would have the apartment to herself. She liked nothing better.

Not that she did not enjoy the company of her uncle and aunt. They were her favorite people. And to them she was more like a daughter than a niece; indeed, she was often mistaken for that owing to her resemblance to her uncle. They had taken her with them to London, Paris and Rome. So many and so fine were their gifts to her she had to refuse some so as not to arouse her father's jealousy of his more successful younger brother. The penthouse was her second home. Her aunt urged her to invite her boyfriends there. The suggestion was that in that rarified atmosphere any young man would be impressed by her connections.

"I haven't got any boyfriends," said Cecily.

The coming of Constance, now two, rather than displacing the niece, drew the three still closer. Cecily felt toward her little cousin like a big sister. And she never felt more at home than when she was alone in possession of the place and entrusted with the care of the child.

Her uncle and aunt were dressed to go. Cecily complimented them on their clothes. The three kissed and the parents left.

Cecily sat little Connie in the highchair and warmed her food, talking all the while. The child listened as round-eyed as a parakeet perched upon a finger. Cecily fed her, and when she had eaten, bathed her. Then she rocked her, crooning lullabies. She sang "Rock-a-bye, baby," "Froggy went a-courting," "Daddy's gone a-hunting to get a bunny rabbitskin to wrap his baby bunting in." She laid the sleeping child in the crib, covered her, kissed her flushed cheek, switched on the nightlight and left her.

After her supper Cecily showered. While drying her hair she sat in darkness by the picture window. It was like looking down upon the stars from the heights of heaven. The warmth and whirr of the hair dryer, the darkness, the distant indistinct glow combined to make her drowsy. Taking her book she went to bed.

Somebody was in the apartment. Through the door, left open for her to hear any cry from the child, came the sounds of somebody moving about. A siren went off in her mind. She must get to the child! She switched off her lamp and got out of bed.

Before she could take a step the overhead light came on. Dazzled by it and in terror she did not at once recognize the man in the doorway. Then, "Uncle Jim!" she cried. "It's you! Oh, thank heaven!" And she rushed into his arms. There she nestled while her quaking slowly subsided.

"I wasn't feeling well," he said. "Norma went on to the opera alone."

She noticed then that he was in pajamas. It was him undressing that she had heard before. He had wanted not to disturb her.

"Oh!" she exclaimed. "You must go to bed and let me take care of you."

"That," he said, "is what I've got in mind. Going to bed and you taking care of me." Pressing her close, he kissed her lips.

She broke free and backed across the room. She was too dazed to be indignant. She could not believe this was happening. The familiarity of the setting made it all the more unreal. How could he have so misjudged her? How could he have so misinterpreted her feeling for him? She had been affectionate but never by word or deed had she invited anything like this.

He advanced, holding out his arms to her. So he had done for years, and in them she had found comfort, love, protection.

"Uncle Jim? Uncle Jim?" she pleaded, trying to call up the man she knew, recall him to himself.

He had miscalculated, looked foolish. He was incensed. His face clouded. She feared he meant to force her into submission. Not much force would be needed. She was too sick at heart to put up any strong defense.

"It's *me,* Uncle Jim. Cecily," she said. Hearing herself, she wondered, Can this be me? She felt she was losing her mind. She was sure he had lost his.

He wavered for an instant and in that pause a way to protect herself occurred to her. She dashed past him, through the door and down the hall.

When he caught up with her she was holding the sleeping child to her breast. He stopped as though stunned by a blow. A mirror had been held up to him and he was appalled at what it showed.

She gave him a minute to recover himself, get his bearings. Then she handed him his child. He took it with a look of gratefulness such as a mother gives the nurse the first time hers is placed in her arms.

# Dead Weight

I AM WHAT IS KNOWN in the antiques trade as a picker. A picker is always on the road looking for finds. Some people pride themselves on being specialists. A specialist is somebody with a one-track mind. Your antiques picker has got to know something about everything: furniture — all periods — porcelain, Oriental rugs, paintings — and he has got to have a sharp eye. He must be able to spot a gem in a junkshop or a "sleeper" in a good one. He must be able to tell the fake from the genuine article.

Without a shop of his own, the picker's customers are dealers. That was how I came to know Kelly. He had been born and brought up in the business and he had inherited an old, established shop, one of the best in the Northeast. Carriage trade. By appointment only. Monthly ads in *Antiques* magazine. I went with something to Kelly only when that something was something. No tchatchkes. Whatever I brought him he bought. He knew I knew what I had — I appreciated that — and he never haggled with me. I appreciated that too. Like everybody else, I like to bargain but not to be bargained with.

Being a picker, and being single, I live in my home on wheels, my camper. I am more or less based in upstate New York, where I was born, but I head south in winter on what I call my Dixie raid, buying as I go, sunning myself down there for a while, then returning north to peddle the merchandise I have found. It's a free and footloose life, and once in a while you make a killing. Like I did when I recognized from my memory of an illustration in a book a self-portrait of Sir Joshua Reynolds in what the fool who owned it, showing off his learning, called a copy of Rembrandt's "Aristotle Contemplating the Bust of Homer." Let the seller beware: that's my motto. I look upon myself as a curator, preserving the beautiful things from the past by separating them from those who don't appreciate them and getting them to those who do. Through my hands have passed items now prominently on display in the Metropolitan Museum of Art. It was to Kelly that I took old Sir Josh.

Like me, Kelly was a bachelor. Thus he would have nobody to come home to after the surgery he would soon be having. He told me about it as I was setting off south this year. I invited him to shut up shop and come out and join me when he was up and about. He would have a change of scene and I would welcome his company. It gets lonely by yourself on the road day after day, and I soon tire of country-western music on the radio down there. I would profit from his expertise.

As arranged, he left a message for me with a dealer friend in Durant. I was to meet him at Dallas–Fort Worth.

I could hardly wait to see Kelly. I had something to show him, and he was going to get a professional kick out of the story that went with it.

I like to wander down back roads, and at old houses, no matter how run down, I stop. In fact, the more run down the better. Being often the first picker in the territory, you make some of your best finds there. I've got a nose like a bird dog, if I do say so myself. On this trip, in darkest Arkansas, I had asked a farmer for permission to camp overnight on his land.

"Make yourself right at home," the man said. "You're too late for supper but come to the house in the morning and eat breakfast with us. We set down to the table at half past six."

What were those hillbillies drinking their coffee out of but Chelsea cups and saucers! Chelsea! Hen's teeth are a dime a dozen compared.

"This is pretty chinaware, ma'am," I commented.

"You like them?" she said. Meaning she didn't. "Why, Lord, them old things been in the family for donkey's years."

To her "old" meant out of fashion, tacky, and longtime ownership of a thing meant you could afford nothing newer.

I said there were people up north who collected old things and that my business was dealing in them.

I emptied my cup and turned it bottom up.

"Um-huh," I managed to say despite my excitement. "Sure enough, there's that little gold anchor, the trademark, that this lady I know collects."

Now for occasions such as this one I carry with me on my travels a stock of trade goods. Like the trinkets traded to the Indians, and worth just about as much. Back in the sticks you find people who don't trust government money, have never seen much of it, haven't even got much use for any, but dangle a gimcrack before them and their eyes light up. To this woman I said that although I dealt generally in old things I had recently seen a set of new china so pretty I just couldn't pass them up. As I reckoned to make a little profit on hers, if she liked mine I would consider a swap with her. And so, for this flea-market junk I got four Chelsea cups and saucers. The fourth one she threw in. The figure I was going to get for them would read like a telephone number. It was Kelly I had in mind.

I had not done quite that well on every transaction along the way but by the time I reached Dallas–Fort Worth I was pulling a rent-a-trailer behind the camper.

The last passengers off the plane trickled through the gate, old folks, people with kids to herd. No Kelly. He must have missed his flight. What to do? I decided to wait on for a while in case a call for me came over the loudspeaker. Maybe he was on the next flight.

Then there came Kelly.

He was in a wheelchair being pushed by an airline attendant. From the knee down his right leg was gone. Across the arms of the chair lay a pair of aluminum crutches.

A bit of surgery he had told me he would be having. "A bit," he said. I knew he was a lifelong diabetic, but you don't have a leg amputated for that. Or so I thought.

My words then came back now to mock me.

"Come out and join me on the road," I said, "when you're on your feet again." What he was on — ha ha! — was his last leg. And that was not all. What was left of him was the color of death.

Imagine shipping yourself out to a friend in that condition! What had I let myself in for? One thing was certain: we were heading nonstop for home. His home. I wanted him off my hands. He looked perishable. And I had already made my haul on this trip.

I had steered us through the tangle of lanes leading from the airport when he said he was tired from the flight and wanted to lie down. I stopped by the side of the road so he could make his way to the bunks in the back. Before going he asked, "Do you know what acetone is?"

On top of the rest he was wandering in his mind. What the hell did that have to do with anything?

I humored him. I said yes, I knew what acetone was. I had used it often in refinishing furniture.

"But why?"

"If you should smell that smell," he said, "it's me."

"What!"

"Yes. And it's a bad sign. If I'm giving off that odor on my breath get me to a hospital."

I kept thinking about that for the next hour, my worries mounting by the mile, until, reaching behind me and opening the door to the living quarters, I called, "Kelly?"

From out of there came fumes you could have stripped nail polish with. There was no answer to my call.

I got him to Parkland Hospital in Dallas where, after coming out of his coma, he spent the next three days in intensive care, then was discharged. Into my intensive care.

Once installed in the van, Kelly took it over. He gave me a list of the things he was permitted to eat and the things he was not permitted. The first list included just about all the things I don't like and the second one all the things I do. But I couldn't prepare different meals for the two of us so I had to share his. He didn't like his diet any more than I did, so a lot of thanks I got for cooking and serving it. A cook whose every meal is greeted with disgust and eaten with distaste cannot be an enthusiastic cook. I have got a sweet tooth but he was forbidden sweets and I couldn't bring myself to have dessert while the poor devil watched me. No, he didn't want a drink before dinner. Or rather, yes, he did want one but he wasn't permitted. Which meant I couldn't have one either. Television to while away the evening? Try watching television when the person supposed to be sharing your enjoyment is staring off into the next world.

On account of his leg Kelly got the lower bunk. That went without saying. But though it was unreasonable of me, the way he took it over without so much as a by-your-leave irked me. All night long he snored. He didn't purr like a cat; he growled like a car stuck in the mud and digging in deeper and deeper. He might have apologized for inconveniencing me. He might have thanked me for my care of him. Instead he took all I did for him for granted and demanded more. Being an invalid, and the only child of old parents, he had been spoiled all his life. I learned that only now because I had never before roomed with him. I had to admit that he was like me in this regard: an old bachelor used to having his own way. Rather than agreeable, he was cranky. He had a way of making me feel I was to blame for all that was wrong with him. I tried to be patient and to make allowances for him, but when I reminded myself that he was crippled and sick I had to ask myself why then had he put himself off on me.

I would just as soon have had him spend his time in the bunk while I drove, but no, he sat in the passenger's seat looking straight ahead. I suppose he thought that as my guest he owed me his company. Some company! Not only did he say nothing, my attempts at conversation seemed to weary him. Try making a comment on the passing scene or a little joke: in response a grunt. He would not have been interested in my story of the Arkansas Chelsea china.

He slept late and tired early, and those big camper vans pulling a trailer just inch along, so our days were shortened and our progress slow. But when, to keep up his spirits, I said on stopping for the night, "Well, friend, we made a hundred miles today," he gave me a look as though what I had left unsaid was, "That much closer to getting rid of you." Which was not altogether off the mark, though I did not enjoy having it thought what with all the trouble I was taking for him.

In short, he was — pardon the expression — a pain in the ass. But then I guess there comes a time in our lives when all of us are. I reckon I owe that lesson to Kelly. If so I owe him this one too: when my turn comes I hope at least I will show that I know I'm a pain in the ass. That's little enough to do by way of compensation.

He being my guest, Kelly got first call on the bathroom in the morning. My wait for my turn was long, for, being handicapped, he was slow at everything. On one of those mornings, in Oklahoma, he was slow even for him. I disliked drawing attention to his disability, but after a while, thinking he might be needing help, needing it badly, for when able he was not shy about asking for it, I rapped on the door and called to him. I made his name a question, as though to say, "You all right in there?" I got no answer. I rapped and called again. Still no answer. I cracked open the door, then I flung it open wide. He was seated on the toilet. Again there was that odor of acetone in the air, but this time he was not in a coma, he was dead.

My cargo was perishable, my disposal problem pressing, yet for much of that day I moved no further than Kelly did. Meanwhile, my thoughts ran as counter to each other as the opposite lanes of a road. I traveled up one and down the other. Impatient as I had been with him before, it goes without saying that I was sorry now for the poor fellow, but I confess I was annoyed with him for putting me in this predicament. "Damn you!" I said. "Couldn't you have waited just a few more days?" I had a suspicion that he had known he was about to die on my hands and had kept it from me.

Something that had happened a couple of days earlier, and which at the time had both puzzled and irritated me, sent me searching among the dead man's effects. I found what I had an inkling I would. But first I found something I was not looking for. My suspicion was doubly confirmed.

What I found first was two unused hypodermic needles along

with two full ampules of insulin. What this meant was that for the last two days Kelly had quit taking his vital medicine. I knew this because three days before I had asked how he was fixed for it. I was as concerned as he was that we not run out. He replied that he had two days' supply left. Seeing his end approaching, he had given himself a last little holiday from that first-thing-in-the-morning jab with the needle.

The second thing I found explained this. On that same day we were passing through a town when Kelly said, "Stop."

"What for?" I asked.

"There's a lawyer's office. I've got a piece of legal business to attend to. A small matter. It shouldn't take long."

"What legal business?" I asked impatiently. To me the only business we had was to make miles, get him back where he belonged.

"It's personal," he said, and I felt corrected. True, I had looked after him, put up with him, but that didn't mean I owned him, could treat him like a child.

I drove as near to the place as I could get and he hobbled to the door. While he was inside I sat at the wheel fuming over this delay.

A few miles farther down the road he said, apropos of nothing, "I haven't got any relatives."

That angered me. I thought he was appealing for my pity, of which I felt I had shown enough already, letting me know there was nobody I could put him off on, that I was stuck with him. What was he to me? He was not my brother nor was I his keeper. Once I got him home, he was on his own. He could well afford to hire people to look after him.

What he had been thinking of was that last will and testament he had just made at the lawyer's office, and letting me know there would be nobody to contest it.

When I found it I was peeved. Taken together with his discontinuing his medicine it meant he had suspected he was about to die on my hands.

The envelope was inscribed with its contents and with specific instructions to me, "To be opened on my death." I did so, and I learned that he had left all his worldly goods to me.

What have I done to deserve this? That question is usually asked as a complaint against misfortune. I asked it because I felt undeserving of my good fortune.

Which, however, did not keep me from enjoying it.

The shop of my own that I had always wanted and could never have afforded was mine. I could give up this life on the road I had lived for so long and settle down in a real home for my old age, and with Kelly's money — my money — hire help to keep it. From now on the pickers could come to me.

I broke out a bottle and toasted my benefactor.

"Don't think that just because he had no family he was obliged to leave anything to you," I lectured myself. "He might have left it all to charity or to his old alma mater." My gratitude grew, and with it grew a sense of self-satisfaction, of my being a better person than I gave myself credit for. Kelly had seen me for what I was. You might say he had seen through me.

I felt good too about a resolution forming in my mind.

Kelly had been born and raised and had lived all his life in his home town. His parents were buried in its cemetery. True, even there he would have nobody to come and lay wreaths on his grave, still it was his native place, and maybe the townspeople, visiting the graves of their kin, might for a few years yet to come say on reading his tombstone, "I remember him." Nobody in Oklahoma would. Getting him home dead would be twice as hard as getting him there half dead, but he had counted on me. It was the least I could to to repay him for all he had done for me.

Lifting my glass in his direction, I said with a lump in my throat, "I'll get you back where you belong, old friend. Leave it to me."

I sat at the table looking at the will and those needles and ampules. Together they constituted the fortune I had come into and the means by which I had come into it. Talk about finds!

However, another drink shone a different light on those items. Through narrowed lids I began to see them as others might. I saw them as evidence on a courtroom table, exhibits A and B. There was sure to be suspicion of foul play. There always is where money is involved. And with me no kin to him. An inquest. An autopsy. Charges maybe. A D.A. running for re-election in a crime-free rural county and needing a little publicity for his campaign. Never mind that the body would show no marks of violence. It would also show no trace of the insulin he had injected himself with every morning of his life until the last two. Him crippled, dependent on me, my prisoner in the van, I could have killed him by withholding from him the medicine on which his life depended and inherited his estate without waiting for nature to take its course. Who in this rotten world of ours would believe that I had looked after him out of the goodness of my heart? Many an innocent man languished in prison. To suspect me they needed a motive.

There it lay.

A fine old house, itself filled with precious antiques, the shop, the land, money in the bank: all that was what I was burning as I burned that will. What the hell! I had never owned anything immovable anyway. And I was not suited to sitting in a shop listening to lid-lifters say, "My grandmother had one just like this."

But how I did curse Kelly! Raising my hopes one minute only to dash them the next. My boozy talk about getting him home to be laid to rest among his ancestors came back now to mock me. I would turn him over for disposal to the first undertaker I came to and go on my way.

Then I thought, whoa! Bury him off down here with only my word as to the manner of his death? Sitting in there on the throne was the most precious object of my career. I had to get him back not to claim my reward but so as not to have it look as though I had done him in.

Meanwhile I too had to do what Kelly had been doing when cut short. I left him in place — no tampering with that solid piece of evidence — reached around him and tore off a length of the paper.

"Shit or get off the pot," I said, but not aloud.

Out of sight in the woods I bared my ass to the elements, feeling put upon, inconvenienced, turned out of my own home. But when I squatted a change of heart came over me. Kelly and I were at that moment both in the same posture. Between us was a vital difference, but that was only a matter of time. I would get him home, and without complaining about it. He would do as much for me. I could thank him that it was the other way round.

I rose feeling relieved in body and soul.

Time was passing, not just by the hour but by the minute, yet to avoid troopers, roadblocks, checkpoints, I kept to the by-ways. Not only did this slow me, so did mapping my route, and time and again I got lost and wound up miles off course. How many herds of dairy cows ambling to the barn at milking time, udders swaying, was I held up by! How many farmers in pickups I got stuck behind! While I was still only barely in sight the natives in some of those parts looked up at me from their out-door occupations as though I was the first pioneer to go by since Dan'l Boone passed through going the other direction.

Pressed as I was, I minutely observed the speed limits, though they are meant to be broken. To trap tourists they lay out stretches of twenty-mile-per-hour zones like strips of flypaper down there. In those hole-in-the-road settlements where the main source of municipal revenue is fines, the out-of-state mo-torist is stopped for exceeding the limit by one m.p.h. The offi-cer will then gauge the depth of your tire treads (the local ga-rage will sell you a new set, though there may be a wait), test your windshield wiper blades (ditto), your directional signals, inspect your driver's license, your registration, your insurance, then — what I feared — search your vehicle for drugs — even for contraband liquor in dry counties.

I had another reason as well for wanting not to be stopped. You can be as queer-looking as a two-headed calf and still there is somebody somewhere who could pass for your twin. Less than a year before I had gone into a Post Office for stamps and there on the wall alongside the rental boxes, wanted for every crime in the book, was Yours Truly to the life. I must have been identified by the postmistress and my license number noted be-cause I was not more than twenty miles down the road when I was overtaken by a trooper, siren blaring. He came at me with his pistol drawn and cocked. I spent the night in the local jail, suspected in addition to all my other crimes of housebreaking owing to the valuables in the van. I had to produce everything but my grandmother's birth certificate before I was let go. Good thing Kelly was not aboard! How was I to know but what my look-alike was still on the loose? If so, then with my passenger as evidence against me I would serve the fellow's life sentence for him.

Meanwhile Passenger was ripening, although I refrigerated him and myself with the air conditioner. I used Renuzit, Lysol Spray. I chewed gum, lots of gum, although I dislike chewing gum. I chewed it for the minty smell. I chewed it until that smell came to seem the one I was trying to get away from. *Dead weight:* that expression, meaning something heavy that lends you no help in lifting and moving it, took on a new meaning for me. Never until now had I looked at undertakers' parlors with longing.

Kelly had stiffened in place. The roughest road did not dislodge him. Even the breakdown of the shock absorbers and the visit to Midas with its hydraulic lift he rode out like a bronco-buster. I checked on him from time to time. "Rodin's Stinker," I, ever the art lover, called him. He would have appreciated that.

I would drive for a few hours, reach a Rest Area, relieve myself in the woods (those places *never* have a comfort station), stretch out on the lower bunk and nap awhile. Never for long. The pressure I was under was not conducive to slumber and sweet dreams. I was driving in my sleep.

I had to do something on that trip I never like to do — I passed up hitchhikers. I enjoy company on the road: it relieves the monotony, keeps you alert. I am outgoing. I am inquisitive by nature. I get their stories out of them. I enjoy doing a good turn that costs me nothing, I appreciate the thanks. Now passing a hiker I would point that I was turning off just down the way. Of course, with my New York license plate, they knew that was a lie.

I tried switching on the radio for a little distraction. I tuned in a local disk jockey with a program called "Golden Oldies." I soon switched it off. It saddened me to reflect that Kelly, whose shop had been filled with the music of Bach and Mozart, would have been glad now to listen to "Lay that pistol down, babe. Lay that pistol down. Pistol-packin' mama, lay that pistol down."

Each state line was a Berlin wall, but with a difference. I both did and did not want to cross it. Not that I wished to tarry a moment longer in the one I was leaving. I blessed my lucky stars at having gotten through it. But the other side was enemy territory, too. Now I had it to get through. No one will ever know just how big America is until he or she smuggles mortal remains fast going bad across it.

Once we were stopped by a traffic director at a crossroads to allow a funeral cortege to turn into our lane. The deceased must have been both prolific and popular, for the procession of mourners was as long as a freight train. Kelly and I coupled on as the caboose. I too switched on my headlights. We went at a solemn pace and the trip to the cemetery gates was long. But while I chafed at the delay, at the same time, following behind a legal corpse with a proper certificate I felt myself comouflaged, a duckling undetected in a hen's brood. I was sort of wistful when they turned off to lay theirs to rest while I was left to carry on alone with mine, and with many a mile yet to go.

Another time we were the ones at the head of a long line of traffic. We were in a No Passing zone and it kept lengthening until it stretched out of sight like a wagon train wending its way.

At last we came to a spot where I could pull off the road and let them pass. What a parade went by! I counted four fire engines, two ambulances, six school buses, eleven cars that with a little restoration would have been called classics up north — all this on a secondary road!

I fell in behind them and proceeded on my way. Pretty soon a line as long as the one ahead had piled up behind me.

We came to the edge of a town. Above the street streamed a

banner proclaiming this to be Windsor's centennial celebration day. A man who would have scaled 240 was directing traffic. All one way. Nobody was leaving town.

Seeing my license plate he stopped everything and came to my window. I rolled it down a crack. I could have heard him just as well through the glass, for he had a voice to shatter it.

"Welcome to Windsor, stranger! Just go down there four blocks, turn right and follow the crowd."

Ahead of me at that intersection stretched an empty street. But I was not going down it any further. Nobody was. The traffic cop there had his arm out like the barrier at a railroad crossing.

Now, as is well known, Southerners are hospitable folks. They have got that reputation to keep up. Southern hospitality can be downright insistent, you might almost say belligerent. A local offers to buy you a drink and you decline, he just may take offense and floor you. The last thing I wanted to do was draw unfriendly attention to myself and certainly not to stir up ill-will by treating these people's festivities with disrespect. Let them think Windsor's centennial celebration was what I had come all the way from New York for. If I tried to get out of town that day I might have been ridden out on a rail.

I parked the van in the pasture at a distance from the other cars. This being a dry county, the first man I met offered me a drink from the bottle in his hip pocket. He inspected it after I handed it back. A token nip would have been an insult to him, a reflection upon my own manhood, and upon the honor of my section of the country, which I was there to uphold.

I was passed from one to another.

"Jeff, Cy, Rory, like you to meet my friend Yank here." And out of the pockets came the bottles.

The parade, with its majorettes, floats, marching band, antique cars, fire companies, after going past, turned down a side street, went around the block and came back and passed in review two more times. Then, after the barbecue, baseball history was made in Windsor that day.

As an honorary citizen of the town, and having not so much as a fifth cousin on the field for me to favor, I was named umpire of the Little League game. I was strictly impartial. I hunkered and peered and whatever the pitch, over whichever of the plates I was seeing, out shot my left hand and forefinger and I yelled, "Ball!" Every runner was safe by a country mile. The only outs were made on caught flys. There were protests at first, but when I kept it up and the crowd caught on, my every call was cheered. Seeing that their parents were on my side the players played along. Kids are brought up to be respectful of their elders down there. Even the protestors addressed me as "sir." I allowed the side to bat through the lineup, then in order to retire them and give the others their turn the next three batters went down on called strikes. The players' short legs were worn out from trotting the basepaths. They were glad to quit when the game ended after three innings in a tie: 26–26. I was carried off the field to the tune of "For He's a Jolly Good Fellow." The only umpire ever so honored. You could look it up.

The festivities continued into the night. It would be another hundred years before Windsor again had something to celebrate. By early evening I was in no condition to drive anyway.

Mighty hospitable people! I wished I had been free to ask, "You folks wouldn't have a nice quiet little cemetery with a vacancy in it somewhere, would you? I've got a friend there in the van with me who could use one." I feel sure they would have said that any friend of mine was a friend of theirs, and that they had no objection to dead Yankees.

*

An old horse will find its way to the barn with the rider asleep in the saddle; my van was that way with yard sales. It would stop for the smallest — you never know. Now I had to keep a tight rein and spur it past them. But at one of the biggest I ever saw, somewhere in Virginia, it balked and would not be prodded on.

I can flit through your average yard sale like a hummingbird among blossoms. But this one: you would have thought the Smithsonian had cleaned out its attic. There was scarcely an item to be passed over without consideration.

"You ought to have been here last week," said the lady in charge.

That spoiled my day but not for long. There were still plenty of pickings. The anything-but-modest home was that of a First Family. Now it had been opened like King Tut's tomb.

There were coin silver spoons. Antique cameras. Old fishing lures. Cut glass. Paperweights. Decoys. Piggybanks. Mechanical toys. Model railways. Jewelry. Just for starters.

Time was passing and I was conscious of it. But whenever I resolved to tear myself away and move on my eye was caught by something else. I wore a path carrying cartons to the van. I filled the space remaining in the trailer. I would have hitched on a second one if I could have. I filled the upper bunk and I wondered how I was going to get to the lower one through all that was stacked on the floor. The lady was half an hour totaling my purchases on her pocket calculator. And Kelly was half a day further from home.

The bathroom in a van like mine was not designed for double occupancy. It was not much roomier than a telephone booth — or a coffin. But I was smelling mighty high myself, and my growth of whiskers, taken with my bloodshot eyes from lack of sleep, was enough to land me in a police lineup.

I considered checking into a motel. But in the first place it would be wondered why anybody with a van would do that. Besides, I could not afford to lose a whole night, and any man who checked out of a room after just long enough for a shower and a shave would surely have been reported. Must have a corpse on his toilet: it shows how obsessed I was that this should seem to me the natural suspicion.

I wanted a bath as never before. Enough to overcome my distaste at joining Kelly. I undressed.

But when I opened the door I almost backed out and closed it. That was what anybody would have done who had intruded upon a live person in a toilet. To do so with a dead one seemed an even greater invasion of privacy. I felt like begging pardon.

To bolster myself I said, "Whose bathroom is this anyway?" It came out sounding rather hollow. For the fact was it seemed to me that my guest had a better claim on it than I did.

I had meant to shower quickly, shave, and make my getaway. But I felt dirty from the inside out, and that spray was a veritable baptism. I splashed like a bird in a birdbath. I sang like one. I sang:

> Ole man Mose done kick de bucket.
> Kick de bucket.
> Buck buck bucket.
> Ole man Mose done kick de bucket.
> Ole man Mose is dead.

I sang:

> A dead man lay deep in his grave.
> He was all down and out.
> The worms crawled in,
> The worms crawled out.
> They crawled all over his dirty snout.

What I was doing is known as whistling past the graveyard. Meanwhile my dead man did not lie in his grave.

I defy anybody to shave with a corpse watching him and not emerge from the experience a changed man. I nicked myself in three places, I was that shaky. My face in the mirror seemed that of a stranger with a resemblance to me. Like the fugitive pictured on the Post Office wall. "Wanted."

Wondering when and where and what my own end would be, I felt sorrier than ever for Kelly. I felt sorry for everybody, but the indignity of it made his death all the more pathetic. He deserved to be stretched out in repose, not slumped on a toilet seat. He would have hung a DO NOT DISTURB sign on the doorknob if he could have. Yet I, whose efforts had all been to keep the body hidden, now felt an urge to exhibit it. Invite people in. Say, "Take a look. There you are. This is what it all comes down to."

I thought how unnoticed you were until you died. You got a moment's attention then. Before stamping your passport and putting you out of sight and out of mind the world wanted to make sure your exit was legal.

We were getting there. We were getting there.

Then somewhere in rural Pennsylvania we limped to a stop with a flat as though we had stubbed a toe. I unhitched the trailer, jacked up the van, only to find that the air had leaked out of the spare. My own was pretty low by then too. I lugged the wheel to the filling station I had passed a mile or so down the road. On my way back I was given a lift. I have found the good Samaritans to be young men who drive cars with bodies as full of holes as a fishnet. This one insisted on changing the tire for me. When the work was done he said shyly, "Mister, I could sure use your john. You mind?" How I wished I could have said, "Make yourself at home!" Instead I had to say it was out of order.

In North Nowhere, New Jersey, we spent an hour on a merry-go-round missing the brass ring, that is to say the entrance to the Garden State Parkway. After that every tollbooth hopper I tossed coins into was another prayer bead counted off.

Crossing the Hudson I renamed it the Styx. Then, "Welcome to New York The Empire State," said the road sign. I felt I had reached the Pearly Gates.

But if the path to those gates is straight and narrow, getting through them is the real squeeze.

My Saint Peter was a state trooper. I was barely over the line when he came after me from out of ambush among the trees. Told what my offense was, I went as rigid as Kelly.

The trooper pointed to the little sticker in the lower left-hand corner of the windshield. It was yellow. It ought to have been blue — that was what they were wearing this year. I had forgotten to have the van inspected before going south.

The justice of the peace in the next village to whom I paid my fine, after lecturing me on the seriousness of my infraction and entering it on my conviction card (one more and my driver's license would be suspended), directed me to an inspection station just down the road. I passed it by. I found a secluded spot and there Kelly and I spent the day. For when your car is inspected the mechanic gets behind the steering wheel to test your lights, your brakes, your directional signals, and the presence in the van of something unburied was marked. We would travel the rest of the way by night. Laying up by day I was able at least to get some sleep.

I have met people down south who have the notion that New York City is New York State. (I have met people from New York City who have that notion, too.) As a native son I can say it isn't so. No matter how you slice it, New York is big. Kelly and I were still not home. We might be on the last lap, but that is the one for which you have to draw on your second wind. I was now both panting and holding my breath. I heard the wheels roll but in the dark you cannot tick off the familiar landmarks and it seemed to me that we were treading in place.

We had had to wait out a few thunderstorms but otherwise the weather had been on our side. I kept in touch by radio with the forecasts, although I had once heard a five-year-old say to her grandfather, who was lamenting that their picnic was going to be rained out, "Papa, haven't you learned yet that those fellows are always wrong?" One meteorologist I tuned in on said, "Well, folks, the temperature has risen twenty degrees in just the last hour and that's only the tip of the iceberg." First laugh I had had in days.

One afternoon I was wakened by a noise like a tank battalion. I looked out to see the tail end of a snowplow. Some eight inches had fallen and it was still coming down thick. In upstate New York about the only time you can count on that not happening is mid-August. It was twenty-four hours before we could get going again.

It will not be misunderstood, I trust, when I say that I enjoyed Kelly's funeral. Not that I danced on his grave, of course. I was somber as befitted the occasion and the crowd and my standing among them. Our story had made the newspaper. The publicity drew a large turnout. They came not to bury Kelly but to praise me. I had become something of a local hero. To my supporters I said that I had done only what they would have done in my place.

When I say "supporters" I refer to my ongoing battle with the law.

The most serious suspicion was murder.

"Kill him!" I exclaimed. "Why would I do that?"

"Maybe he snored," said the police lieutenant.

As I have said, he did. I colored.

I waived my right to counsel. Why hire someone to defend me when I had nothing to hide? I was requested to take a polygraph test and, would you believe, I failed it! Just being asked such questions is enough to make your heart pound and your blood pressure rise.

How I sweated! And sweating is one of the things they measure, being supposed to give you away as a liar. But practice makes perfect, and I passed the second test, which I requested.

No motive for murder could be established. The police were disappointed but that count was dropped. Now I am charged with unlicensed transportation of human remains. Failure to seek medical assistance. Failure to report a death. Violation of the sanitary code. Endangerment to public health. Does this mean, I wonder, however I fare in New York, that I face these same charges in every state along the way on my next Dixie raid?

# Be It Ever
# So Humble

ON GETTING UP in the morning the first thing Lily Harper did, even before putting in her denture, was to make the bed. She boxed the corners and smoothed the cover as neatly as a soldier. Lily was tidy by nature; she was also tidy out of terror. Her daughter Elizabeth might burst in at any hour, inspect the room like a sergeant in the barracks, and an unmade bed was all the evidence needed for her to declare that Lily was no longer able to look after herself.

Not look after herself! If ever there was an "efficiency apartment" hers was it. Three hundred and sixty square feet of floor space: who could not keep that clean? The place was as cozy as a cubbyhole. Turn from the hotplate and there was the sink. After a meal of hers there was one pot, one plate, one knife and fork to wash. Waste disposal? She generated no waste. Nothing was ever left on her plate. Her laundry, which she did often, again both because she was naturally neat and out of fear of Elizabeth's fault-finding, fit in the lavatory. As for the occasional cockroach, who in the city was free of those? One of Lily's park-bench acquaintances reported seeing them in the most respected hospital. But just let Elizabeth spot one and it was, "Mama, you are no longer able to look after yourself."

Cockroaches led to her health.

"Mama, you've grown thin."

"I have not grown thin. I always was. The one time I wasn't was when I was carrying you. Much obliged for your concern, but I'm fine."

Moreover, she had Mr. Ellis to keep watch on her. There was his rap now, dependable as an alarm clock.

Through the closed door Lily said, "Good morning, Mr. Ellis."

"Good morning, Mrs. Harper."

"How are you today, Mr. Ellis?"

"Very well, thank you, Mrs. Harper. Yourself?"

"Very well, thank you."

"Have a nice day."

"Thank you, Mr. Ellis. And you too."

The boyfriend down the hall, Elizabeth called Mr. Ellis. She suspected that Lily and he were in league to keep out of their children's clutches. She was right, they were.

This morning Lily was going shopping. Today it was to be the A & P. Unlike most housewives, who favored one market because there they knew where to find the things on their list, Lily spread her patronage over them all. For her, shopping was not a chore, it was an outing, an adventure. She never made a list. Nor did she shop, as did many on fixed incomes, adding up their purchases on a pocket calculator as they went along so as to stay within their budgets. She pushed her cart down the aisles taking from the shelves whatever suggested itself.

Yet she was nothing if not choosey. Before settling on an eggplant or a head of lettuce she considered and rejected half a dozen. To win her approval a cut of meat, a ham, a turkey must undergo a thorough inspection. She was not immune to a bargain, but quality, not cost, was her prime consideration. She mistrusted off-brands.

It was evident to anyone watching her that Lily was a savvy

shopper. Her age too testified to experience. The assurance with which she selected items encouraged elderly men, new to keeping house for themselves, and indecisive young apprentice house-wives to ask her advice. Being in no hurry, she was generous with it. When asked what one did with artichokes, avocados, parsnips, she explained at length. Although she herself was un-concerned about prices, she sympathized with those who were. This led to many friendly chats.

Caravans of jet planes made of today's supermarket an em-porium that put the world at one's fingertips. They had abol-ished the seasons. Somewhere on the globe, mere hours away, the blush was on the grape, the melon was sweet on the vine. There were fresh figs in February, tomatoes in March. There were potatoes from Idaho — ah, Idaho! snowpeaked mountains, ski lifts; dates from Saudi Arabia — sand, camels, veiled women. Danish trout, Polish ham, Dutch cheese, Mexican enchiladas. The market was like the Garden before the Fall, with all the tempting goods in reach.

When her cart could hold no more Lily took from it a can of soup and a loaf of bread and, leaving it parked in an aisle, went to the quick checkout. As she was paying for her purchases she felt a grip on her shoulder.

"Come with me," said the man.

"Mama," said Elizabeth. "Mama, I'm talking to you. This is it. You hear me? *This* is IT. I have never been so humiliated. How that man lectured me! Well, I don't blame him. Have you no idea how many man-hours are lost in putting all those things back in their places on the shelves? He told me that every store manager in town has been on the lookout for you. Well, you've been nabbed. Your little shopping sprees are a thing of the past. They've got you on videotape. You can never show your face in a supermarket again. I'll give you until tomorrow to pack your things. You're off to the home. And high time," she concluded with a sniff at her surroundings.

Lily knew the home. When newly widowed she had volunteered a day's work a week there, until she could stand it no more.

"Home" was a cruel misnomer. Home was just what it was not. It was a graveyard full of living ghosts. Home might be nothing more than a sparsely furnished room, but so long as it was yours and yours alone you were you.

Pallid as creatures that lived under planks, the inmates were propped in rows along the walls to drowse. The waking and howling of one would set them all howling like the dogs of a neighborhood. The bedridden stared at the ceiling. Those who were able stalked the corridors, their split gowns exposing their backsides, a look in their eyes as though searching for the selves they had lost. The most pitiful were those who knew where they were. "Get me out of this place. Get me out of here," Lily had heard them plead with their relatives. Sharp instruments, cords, even bedsheets were kept from them. During Lily's time there one inmate drowned herself in a toilet bowl. Another suffocated his screeching roommate with a pillow.

"Be ready for me at ten," said Elizabeth.

The bed was made. Now Lily sat waiting in her coat, hat and gloves.

There came a rap on the door.

"Good morning, Mr. Ellis," she called.

"Good morning, Mrs. Harper."

"How are you this morning, Mr. Ellis?"

"Very well, thank you, Mrs. Harper. Yourself?"

"Very well, thank you."

"Dress warmly if you're going out today."

Too softly for him to hear she said, "Goodbye, dear Mr. Ellis."

She allowed him time to return down the hall. Then she stood and took a last look around the room.

"Goodbye," she said, as though to herself.

So that it need not be broken open she left the door unlocked behind her.

# A Heart in
# Hiding

IT WAS HIS MORNING to make breakfast. They took turns. For today he had in store a treat. This being a Sunday they would lie abed late, reading the paper over their tea. Not that it mattered anymore what day of the week it was nor what hour they got up, but you felt less guilty lazing while others were not at work either. Leaving her sleeping, he stole downstairs, clinging to the rail, testing his footing before proceeding. The old stairs creaked, and so did his joints.

He got the paper from the porch. While around the world war raged, here the scent of lilacs perfumed the air and a wren sang his love song.

In the kitchen the cat stirred from sleep, stretched herself and yawned. As he poured a saucer of milk she twined around his legs.

"Puss, Puss, always underfoot," he said. "Someday you're going to trip me, I'll fall, break my leg and be taken to the hospital. Then won't you be sorry?"

Having heard this many times before, Puss purred.

He laid out the makings of the meal. As he was peeling the caps of the mushrooms an old song tapped at the door of his memory. He welcomed it like a long-lost friend. He had picked it up from a street singer on the Via Partenope during that sab-

batical year in Naples long ago. Now to recall the words he had
first to translate them.

> I'll build myself a house in the middle of the ocean
> Made of peacock feathers.
> *Me voglio fa na casa mmiez' 'o mare*
> *Fravacata de penne de pavune.*
> Of silver and gold I'll make the grates
> And of precious stones the balconies.
> *D'argento e d'oro voglio fa lli ggrare*
> *E de prete preziose lli balcune.*
> When my Nennella appears
> Everyone will say:
> "Now the sun has risen!"
> *Quanno Nennella mi se va affacciare*
> *Ognuno dice, ognuno dice:*
> *"Mo sponta lo sole!"*
> *Trallalallalla llallarallalla.*

Who said his memory was going bad!

He put the mushrooms and the tomato slices in one pan of
slowly simmering butter, the kippers in another, set the kettle
on to boil and spooned the tea into the pot.

Climbing the stairs, balancing the tray, he raised his voice
and sang again the song's last verse. She would waken to fond
Italian memories.

He was winded when he gained the landing. He paused for
breath, then went down the hall and entered the bedroom singing the refrain: *Trallarallalla lla . . . la . . . la . . .*

She was dead.

When the body had been taken away he sat awaiting the on-
slaught of grief like a man in the electric chair. But the switch
was not thrown. He felt nothing. Nothing whatever. He shook

his head like shaking a watch to make it tick. It responded with
*tra la la la . . .*

Without her it was as though the day had not begun. The
house was silent. Always before it had been filled with music
every waking hour. There was a radio in the bedroom, another
in the kitchen, a player and records by the hundreds in the den.
He sometimes called her his Anna Livia Plurabelle, and quoted,
"'Sea shell ebb music wayriver she flows.'" She liked all kinds:
symphonic, chamber, opera, jazz, the popular songs of their
youth. Now it was as though the house had been submerged.

After forty-two years it must have come to seem to him that
their marriage would just go on and on. It ought to have been
the very opposite with each passing day. But when he warned
himself that it could not go on forever like this, it was more to
scare himself into a fuller appreciation of his good fortune than
it was out of conviction. It was not that he took his wife for
granted, but rather that he could not imagine — could scarcely
even remember — life without her, and he could neither remember nor imagine not living. He had marveled at how it was
that of all the potential pairs on this earth he and she had found
each other as unerringly as lock and key. Throughout his working life as a professor he had been much at home; since his
retirement they were together at all times, seldom out of each
other's call. To accept the sudden end of so permanent a part-
nership was impossible.

It was said that after the fall of the blade of the guillotine and
the severance of the head from the trunk the eyes went on flut-
tering and the limbs twitching — something similar seemed to
have happened to him. He watered the plants, took out the garbage, emptied the machine of yesterday's dishes. In this state of
suspended animation he spent the day, waking like a sleep-
walker from time to time to wonder how he had gotten where

he was. The inappropriateness and triviality of his thoughts appalled him. Had he undergone some atrophy of the heart, hardening of the arteries? He would have been lost without her, he used to say. Now he was lost. And even telling himself this did not flush his heart from hiding.

He had forgotten the cat. It was late, and having been kept waiting long past her dinner hour, she clambered up his leg as he diced the raw liver.

He had no idea what time it was, for time had stopped. He told himself he ought to go to bed. He switched off the lights. But three steps up the stairs he realized that he was going to bed alone, would wake alone. He turned back and went to the living room. The cat came and leapt on his lap.

Lulled by her purring he grew drowsy. Up to his last waking moment there kept running in his mind that refrain *tra la la la* . . .

The blood pressure pill he took the next morning was the last one in the bottle. He went into town to have the prescription refilled.

As he was leaving the drugstore he saw an item for sale that stopped him in the aisle. It was a bamboo backscratcher. The sight brought to mind the countless times he had asked her to scratch his back. He could feel again the touch of her fingers, the soothing relief. "Higher. There. Ahh . . ."

His tears flowed and, grateful for his grief, he shook with sobs.